PRAISE FOR MICHELE CLARK MCCONNOCHIE

Very well written in concise language and divided into 63 chapters of 2/3 pages each. You can pick it up and read for ten minutes then come back, but you won't—it is too exciting for that. Believable fantasy and behind it all is a sharp sense of humour that even adults will appreciate. A book that demands to be read aloud to children from 8—13 years old.

Bob Docherty, Bob's Books, NZ

An imaginative and light-hearted fantasy adventure novel that has bags of energy, humour and originality. This is a book to be enjoyed by children aged 9-12, as well as their parents. 85%.

The Book Reviewers.

The Sagas continue to be extremely well written with delightful animal characters that show real passion for the love of them! These books show compassionate love of fellow man, too, with a great mystery and goal involved! Easy to read, too, with short chapters which is great for children! Can hardly wait for the final Saga!

Pete & Peggy, Amazon 5* Review

The funniest part of the book is how the group manages to get themselves kidnapped by goblins and how they escape using an uncooperative but accommodating flying carpet.

Gauri Bhandari, NZ Booklovers

I'm pleased this is the first book in a series because I really enjoyed reading it. It made me laugh a lot. Even though I hadn't met Sabrina before in other books, I felt like I knew her pretty quickly. I'm not saying which fairy tales get touched upon in this book because that's a fun part of the story. There is a good mix of humour, great peril, sibling disagreement, and some aww moments too. It's gone on my digital reread bookshelf!

Nayu's Reading Corner

THE UNCOMFORTABLE GLASS SLIPPERS

UNCOMFORTABLE GLASS SLIPPERS
the STRANGE SAGAS of SABRINA SUMMERS

SAGA
2

MICHELE CLARK MCCONNOCHIE

NEW YORK

LONDON • NASHVILLE • MELBOURNE • VANCOUVER

The Uncomfortable Glass Slippers

The Strange Sagas of Sabrina Summers, Saga 2

© 2020 Michele Clark McConnochie

Published in New York, New York, by Morgan James Publishing. Morgan James is a trademark of Morgan James, LLC. www.MorganJamesPublishing.com

ISBN 9781642796872 paperback
ISBN 9781642796889 eBook
Library of Congress Control Number: 2019943706

Cover Design by:
Rachel Lopez
www.r2cdesign.com

Front Cover Illustration by:
Donna Murillo

Interior Design by:
Christopher Kirk
www.GFSstudio.com

Morgan James is a proud partner of Habitat for Humanity Peninsula and Greater Williamsburg. Partners in building since 2006.

Get involved today! Visit
MorganJamesPublishing.com/giving-back

ALSO BY MICHELE CLARK MCCONNOCHIE

THE STRANGE SAGAS OF SABRINA SUMMERS SAGA 1
THE UNCOOPERATIVE FLYING CARPET

AND COMING SOON

THE STRANGE SAGAS OF SABRINA SUMMERS SAGA 3
THE UNCONTROLLABLE SLINGSHOT

DEDICATION

This book is dedicated to my mum, Hazel Gibson

I love her heaps and am blessed to have had her love and
support in all that I have done in life, wherever I am
in the world. She has always been there for me and
I am hugely grateful to this amazing, brave, clever woman.

ACKNOWLEDGEMENTS

Writing books can be a bit lonely, not to mention quite boring! Luckily, I had lots of company and love along the way and I want to thank my friends and family for all their support.

My husband, Brent, was a fantastic sounding-board, collaborator and editor and I love him heaps.

A massive 'thank you' to my mum Hazel, my dad David, my step-dad Michael – I am so proud of my mum who has always been incredibly supportive of me and I am thankful for her help and love. Also, thanks to my brother, Russell, sister-in-law Jeab, and godmother Peggy – you have all always been there for me and I can't thank you enough. And a very special 'thank you' to my niece Erin Clark who inspired me so much that I wrote my first ever children's stories for her when she was busy growing up into the amazing, mature woman she is today.

Many people kindly donated their names to characters in this trilogy. Although the characters are nothing like the real people (and cat), I was proud to be able to honor them in this way. Thank you to Twinkle, Hazel and Michael Gibson, Dave Clark, LuAnne Underwood Autry, Peggy Lee Underwood Hornsby, Meera, Olive Saunders, Persis Clark, Don McConnochie, Muriel McConnochie, Heath and Nathan Matavuso-Lowe, Yvonne Tissington, Yvonne Lowe, Russell Clark and Ellie Tomsett.

I love the fabulous front cover of this book, don't you? It was designed by the very talented Donna Murillo of DHMDesign and I am grateful to her, and to Sarah Nisbet of Inkshed Editorial who did a brilliant first edit of this book.

I am extremely grateful to Wendy Busby who helped me understand dyslexic-readers and the character of Rory, and to Esther Whitehead, Managing Trustee of the Dyslexic Foundation of New Zealand who was so helpful when I contacted her for advice.

I am very lucky and proud that this book was accepted by Morgan James Kids to be published. Many, many thanks to everyone there.

And finally, did you know that The Uncomfortable Glass Slippers is the second book in a trilogy? All three books together are called The Strange Sagas of Sabrina Summers. It came from a short story I wrote for my stepdaughter when she was a little girl, and the character of Sabrina is inspired by her. This trilogy is dedicated to Steph McConnochie, love her lots.

However old you are, if you want to write a book or some short stories, then you can ask your friends and family for their support too.

PROLOGUE

It was a terrible day for a birthday party. The rain slanted down, driven stinging into the faces and hands of the partygoers as they jumped around on the jungle gym at a small park across the street from a pretty church.

The man they used to call the Beast with Nine Fingers, but who was now known as the Beast with Eight Fingers, stood behind a tree. He watched the small group of boys playing and yelling loudly. They were being looked after by two adults—a man who was snuggled into a heavy raincoat and a woman who had her arm around his waist. The Beast stared with pure hatred at the woman. She wriggled her shoulders as if she could sense the presence of something evil. She glanced behind her to see what was making her feel like this, and the Beast dodged behind his tree again.

He was sure she hadn't seen him but she had sensed him. He had to be careful—you could never trust a witch.

He flexed the fingers on his left hand open and closed. The cold, wet weather made his hand ache where two of his fingers had been accidentally chopped off. That's right, two fingers—talk about careless.

He quickly slipped into his disguise and stepped out from behind the tree. He walked over to the couple, holding out a plastic shopping bag which held a brightly-wrapped present.

"How's the birthday boy?" he called cheerfully as he got closer. A red-headed boy waved across at him, but didn't pause in his rough game of chase.

"Heath!" shrieked the boy. "Nathan's over by the monkey bars. Get him!" And in a splash of puddles they were gone.

"He's growing up, Dave," said the Beast. "What is he now, eight?" The boy's father nodded.

"That's right. And Sabrina is almost thirteen too. Where does the time go?" He shook his head, surprised as all parents are at how fast his two children were growing up.

The Beast thought about what he had heard. Time was running out. He needed to do something about those kids—and he needed to do it fast. He knew that they had found one of the magic objects, but the other two were still available to him. Yes, he needed to move quickly. While he was thinking about his plan, he decided to have a little fun. He pulled a tiny box from his pocket, its surface worn from how often he had used it. It was wooden and had the words 'Property of WW' carved into it. He opened it and a white mist slid out and swirled through the air. The Beast lifted his right hand and flicked it as if he was flicking something from his fingers, something gross that he had found in a nostril perhaps. The white mist shifted, following the direction of his gesture. A sudden gust of wind sprang up and rattled the branches and leaves on a tree so that a great spray of water went all over the woman.

"Oh dear, Bridget," said the Beast, faking his concern. "Are you OK?" But he could not stop a small smirk from twitching his lips under his mustache.

CHAPTER
1

You know how you read in books that someone is so terrified that their blood runs cold? Well, I can tell you now that cold, runny blood is a real thing.

I stared in knee-knocking fear at the woman standing right in front of me. I was too shocked to move. Next to me were my BFF Persis Perkins and my frenemy Olive Ayres. We shuffled a little closer to each other, just to feel safer. How could she be in our school? We thought we had escaped from her when we had left Dralfynia and come back home.

We were standing in the narrow corridor that ran the length of Melas Middle School. Down one side of the corridor were rows of lockers with gaps in between them for classroom doors. The other side had windows that overlooked the schoolyard. Unfortunately, we were one floor up and the windows were always locked. Behind us it was a long, long way to the stairs that would be our only chance of escape. Even if we turned and ran, she could easily catch us.

We were trapped. We were trapped by a witch—a witch who was dressed in a black pantsuit right now, but still a witch.

The woman standing in front of us stretched her face into what she thought was a smile. Weeooow. What a smell. Her teeth were rotten and green, the result of living in a cottage made from gingerbread and candy and snacking on her furniture, I guess.

"Hello Sabrina Summers," she said. "Hello other girls." She took a step toward us, reaching into a pocket and pulling out a stick.

I didn't think I'd be able to move, but at the sight of the stick we all took a step back. What was she going to do with it? Hit us?

She took another step forward. Her legs were longer than ours and in one pace she was on top of us, looking down.

"Nice to see you again," she said, smirking and flicking her wrists out in front of her as if she was warming up. Her eyes were chips of ice.

"Not nice to see you again, Witchy Wu," I said. My voice came out squeaky and choked—I had been trying for tough and grown up. She ignored my words but Olive and Persis moved slightly away from me.

"Toads, perhaps? Or shall I turn you into the slimy, cottage-eating slugs that you really are?"

Ah. She wasn't going to hit us with the stick then—it was her magic wand.

I cleared my throat. Perhaps I could scream for help? But her gaze held me in its power, making my throat tighten and my mouth go dry. My scream withered away. All I could do was stare into her eyes—one green and one black. We had learned that all witches had eyes of different colors and hers glittered with excitement. She was enjoying how scared we were.

"On the other hand," she hissed, "I think I'll just eat you raw." She lunged at me, her sharp, red fingernails were clawed to slash at my face, but her hand swiped through my hair, barely missing my cheek as I dropped to my knees. Her sudden attack was vicious. She meant business. There was nothing for it, we would have to make a dash for it.

I opened my mouth to yell to Persis and Olive to run, then I spotted something behind Witchy Wu. Instead of yelling out, I snapped my mouth shut again and rose to my feet. A door to one of the rooms farther down the corridor had opened and I could see the figure of a man striding in our direction.

"Ah, Ms. Wu," he cried joyfully. "Splendid, splendid, splendid," he exclaimed. We usually tried to avoid Principal McPhail. He was one of those grown-ups who talk very loudly, is always very excited about everything, and likes to say the same thing three times in a row. He exhausted us with all that puppy-like enthusiasm and of course we nicknamed him Principal McFail. Right now though, I was never so happy to see him.

He clapped his hand firmly on the shoulder of the woman we knew as Witchy Wu and I was pleased to notice that she flinched.

"Getting to know some of our student body I see," he boomed, smiling as widely as if he had just won a million dollars. "Let me introduce you," he continued. "Girls, this is Ms. Wu, who will be teaching cookery and will be your Home Room teacher. Ms. Wu, this is …" Then his forehead went all wrinkly as he tried to remember our names.

"Olive, Persis and Sabrina," said Olive helpfully. I rolled my eyes. Although the two of us had started to make friends during our recent adventure in Dralfynia, we still irritated each other. I mean, seriously, what kind of girl helps out the principal?

"That's right, Persis, well done," said Principal McPhail. I couldn't help it; I giggled. Poor Olive, now all the praise would go to Persis, who was blushing.

"Is something funny, Olive?" he asked me. Oh dear. I giggled again. Should I correct him? Persis, who was rolling her own eyes at me now, seized the moment to come to our rescue.

"No, nothing, sir," she said, as she grabbed my arm. "We'll leave you and Wit— I mean, um, Ms. Wu to um … well, whatever you guys do, and we'll get to class," she gabbled pulling me toward the stairs and away

from them both. Olive followed us and we practically ran down the corridor, skidding on the polished linoleum.

We didn't head to class, though. We headed straight for the tradi-
tional place to hide and talk about our problems—the girls' bathroom.

CHAPTER
2

"Ohmygosh—Ohmygosh—Ohmygosh. What are we going to do?" whispered Olive. She was practically crying. I didn't blame her. Now I had stopped my nervous giggling, I felt like crying too. But I couldn't give way to tears. We had only just survived an accidental journey to a strange land with my little brother Rory and a unicorn with gas problems named Clyde. I had learned one thing during that adventure. Whether I liked it or not, I was the leader of our strange gang, and that meant no tears for me.

Persis pulled down the toilet seat and sat on it. We had all huddled into the cubicle at the furthest end of the bathroom and locked the door behind us while we decided what to do.

"Do you think Principal McPhail's OK?" she asked with panic in her voice. "I mean, I know he's kind of a pain, but she's a wicked witch after all."

"Oh sure, he'll be fine," I said but it was more to be reassuring than because I actually believed it.

"Why is she here? What does she want from us?" Persis continued. She gnawed at her bottom lip while she thought about it. "I mean, we ate quite a lot of her house, but this is taking revenge a bit far, isn't it?" she said.

"Well, we—OK, I—accidentally chopped off a finger belonging to that prince she works for, so she might be mad about that," I suggested. Olive nodded, thinking about my words. We were starting to calm down a little, feeling safe now that we were out of sight of Witchy Wu. We thought back to our recent and very strange saga in the extremely weird land of Dralfynia.

"We did more than just eat her house and accidentally chop off the prince's finger," Olive said. "We escaped from right under her nose when those goblins had kidnapped us for her, and then we took some of their treasure and threw it at them. Plus, we stole the magic flying carpet and brought it back here." We fell silent, remembering. Ruggy, as Rory had named the flying carpet, was the most uncooperative flying carpet ever. He behaved like a naughty pony and had tried to buck us off him lots of times, but when we needed him, he had saved our lives too.

Olive continued to speak slowly as she worked it out in her head, her pretty face twisted with concentration. She ran her fingers through her glossy chestnut hair as she thought. When she took her hands away, there was not a hair out of place. How does she do that?

"Of course," she said, snapping her fingers excitedly. "Ruggy is one of the three magic objects that whoever wants to be the ruler of Dralfynia has to have." Persis and I nodded. We had made a friend there, a boy called Aidan, who had explained that, along with Ruggy, there was also a pair of glass slippers and a slingshot. If the prince who was Witchy Wu's boss wanted to become king, he needed all three of those things—including the one we had.

Olive looked at us.

"It's Ruggy," she said firmly. "She's here for Ruggy. I bet that Beast with Nine Fingers/prince guy sent her here to get it."

"Beast with Eight Fingers," I corrected her. She was right, of course. She usually was. Persis was the muscles, Olive was the brains and I was the leader of our strange group.

"We're going to have to hide Ruggy," I said, thinking hard. "Then maybe Witchy Wu'll just go back to Dralfynia." Olive shook her head.

"If you hide Ruggy anywhere in Melas, they'll never leave us alone," she pointed out. "The Beast needs Ruggy and he won't stop looking for him." Darn it. She was right again.

"Maybe," said Persis, "she's already turned Principal McPhail into a frog." Olive and I looked at her. She lifted her hands, her palms upwards and dropped them. "It might not be such a bad thing? A principal who could only croak and not talk?"

Olive carried on as if Persis had never spoken. "There is one thing we could try," she began. "But I'm not sure what you'll think of it …" As we waited for her to carry on, the door to the bathroom creaked open and we heard brisk footsteps rat-a-tat-tatting across the tiles. We froze, hardly daring to breathe. It was in the middle of a period. Apart from us, there shouldn't be any kids out of the classrooms.

As slowly and carefully as I could, I dropped to my hands and knees. To give me more room, Olive slid along into the tiny gap between the toilet and the cubicle wall and Persis drew up her knees so that her feet were on the seat.

I peeped under the gap at the bottom of the cubicle. I saw a pair of black shoes with shiny buckles.

Guess who?

CHAPTER 3

Ihat's right. It was Witchy Wu. I flapped my arm around to let the others know they had to be quiet, and I kept my face glued to the gap. I didn't dare move, even though it was uncomfortable and probably unhygienic too. If I twisted my neck, I could manage to see as far up as her waist.

She didn't seem to be looking for us. She wasn't checking the cubicles. Instead, she stood by the sinks and started to speak to herself. I listened hard, terrified that she was going to cast a spell.

From the way her arms moved it looked like she was holding something, but it was too high for me to see it. After a minute, I realized that whatever the thing was, she was talking to someone through it and not reciting an enchantment. At first, I thought that she had a cell phone, but they were banned in school hours. That reminded me of our own sneaky cell phones—oopsy, I hoped that none of them would go off while we were trapped in the cubicle!

"Yes, as I said, I have made contact Your Highness," she whispered. There was a squawking sound and I couldn't make out the reply, but I stiffened as I guessed that she was talking to the Beast himself. I knew that only people who were princesses or princes were usually called "Your Highness".

"No, they don't suspect a thing at the school," she continued. She dropped one of her hands as she spoke and I could see her take a big sugar-covered donut from her pocket and sneakily eat bites of it in between talking. My nose twitched as I caught a whiff of it. It smelled wonderful. Raspberry jelly, I thought. My mouth filled with water and I clenched the muscles in my stomach as hard as I could so that it wouldn't rumble and give us away.

"I agree Your Highness," she mumbled through a mouthful of donut and wiped her fingers on her pants. "If the mouse is correct and they brought the rug here with them, then they must have it in the Summers' home. It is best to wait for the boy's party on Saturday. The house will be empty when they go to the park. I can sneak in and ... shush! I hear something."

In spite of all my efforts, my stomach had suddenly gurgled loudly. I felt Olive give me a warning nudge with her foot, but it was too late.

There was a click as Witchy Wu broke off the connection. As she dropped her hand, I could see that she was holding a small, jeweled mirror. It was the kind that women have in their purses so they could check their makeup. My mind whirred. She had been talking to someone on a compact mirror? Maybe it was a phone disguised to look like a mirror. Then I remembered Olive telling us that she had seen a magic mirror in Dralfynia. Communicating by mirror must be something that Dralfynians did. I mentally clicked my fingers as I worked it out. This must be a mobile magic mirror, the Dralfynian version of our own cell phones.

That was actually pretty cool and I wondered where I could get one but I didn't have time to consider it for long because Witchy Wu was starting to move around, listening for the sound she'd heard. As I watched, she approached the cubicle nearest to the door and suddenly kicked it open. It banged, shattering the silence.

"Come out, come out, wherever you are," she sang. Then we heard her start to walk slowly but deliberately to the cubicle next to the one we were hiding in. Again, she kicked open the door, letting it smack back against the wall with a judder.

"Two down, one to go," she called out. "I know where you are now, my tasty treats."

Abruptly the bell for recess shrilled through the quiet room, making us all jump. I banged my head on the bottom of the cubicle door and gave a little yelp. The door to the bathroom was flung wide and a dozen chattering girls of all ages surged into the room.

I could tell from the shrieks and giggles that they were pretty surprised to see a teacher in their bathroom. I heard the sound of Witchy Wu's footsteps as she left the room. The girls were even more surprised when—one after the other—Olive, Persis and I filed out of the same cubicle and, red-faced, slipped out of the bathroom as fast as we could.

CHAPTER
4

We managed to make it through the rest of the school day by staying back as long as possible in each class we had and then running to the next as fast as we could, skidding in just as the teacher was shutting the door. At lunchtime, we raced into the canteen, grabbed some food and then ran to the yard so we could sit together outside, even though it was cold and drizzly. We pulled our jackets closer around us to keep out the worst of the bad weather.

We got some strange looks from friends and not just because of the weather—people were surprised to see Olive and me sitting together. The other kids knew we didn't really like each other. Neither of us had held back when we were talking about the other behind her back. I felt ashamed now and I think Olive did too. However intrigued they were though, no one came to join us. The warm, dry canteen was too tempting.

"So, what are we going to do?" Persis picked up the conversation we had been having in the girls' bathroom. Hmmm. A good question. I turned to Olive.

"Hey, before Witchy Wu came into the bathroom, you were going to say something. What was it?" I asked her. I was surprised to see her normally beautiful, creamy skin suddenly go red and blotchy.

"Oh, um, well," she said. She was really flustered and it made me a bit suspicious. I narrowed my eyes as I looked at her.

"I was thinking maybe we could tell your mom about it," she said very quickly. "You know, her being another witch and everything. Maybe she could help us."

"She's not my mom," I said. I was trying to be all calm and leader-ish, but I know that I had spat out my words because I saw Olive wipe her cheek. "She's my stepmom and I don't trust her," I carried on, my own face going red and blotchy too. "My Uncle Don already warned me against her," I pointed out. Uncle Don was my hero; my brother Rory's too. Well, what kids wouldn't love an uncle who was a traveling magician and could do fantastic card tricks?

I could tell by Olive's expression that she wanted to object but I cut her off.

"Did you see the notice that came round? We're supposed to have a special Home Room meeting at the end of today to welcome her," I said. "Let's skip school instead. We need to avoid Witchy Wu, and we could try to come up with a plan."

As soon as the words "skip school" were out of my mouth, we felt as if someone was listening to us. Like a trio of meerkats, we stretched up our necks and looked about us. From where we sat, we were hidden from the canteen but if we tried hard, we could look up and see who was at the teachers' table in the window.

We saw the principal and Witchy Wu. Although Mr. McPhail seemed to be talking a lot, Witchy Wu was ignoring him. Instead she stared out of the window in our direction, while ripping the ends from skinny sachets of sugar and pouring them into her mouth, one after another.

Watching her eat all that sugar made me crave broccoli, and that was saying something.

As soon as the bell rang for the last period of the day, we were ready to put into action our plan to go make a plan.

We pushed against the tide of kids all heading to their Home Rooms, getting a few grumbles as we went. For the first time ever in my life, I was skipping school.

CHAPTER 5

We met in the field opposite my house. It was where we had been when we first accidently got sent to Dralfynia. It was also where Clyde the enormous Clydesdale horse lived. We felt better when we were around Clyde; he was so big and he always made us feel safe, but in spite of his comforting presence, and although we talked and talked, we just went round in circles. Olive kept insisting we talk to Bridget. I kept saying no. Persis kept making silly suggestions like running away with my Uncle Don and joining his traveling magic act; or capturing Witchy Wu, taking her to the principal's office and using karate to force her to tell the truth (she planned to quickly learn karate, which she's been dying to do for ages).

I shook my head, feeling frustrated, and stroked Clyde's great neck to make me feel better and because he liked it.

"You know that grown-ups never listen to kids," I pointed out to her. "Especially Principal McPhail," I said. Persis nodded; that was true. Then she tickled Clyde under his chin. He tilted his head up to give her better access.

"Good old Clyde," said Olive, moving to join us. He whinnied. "Do you think he knows he's a unicorn back in Dralfynia?" she wondered.

I stared at him. His mane and tail were mostly white but his coat was brown with white splotches. He was a big, powerful horse, not at all like the kind of unicorn you see in books. And, if you gave him apples, he broke wind. A lot. In fact, his gas had saved us from a bat attack after Witchy Wu had us chased through Scary Forest after she caught us eating her gingerbread cottage.

His brown eyes were soft, but seemed to me to be full of intelligence. "I think that if Clyde could talk, he'd tell us exactly what to do," I said. "I think that Clyde is one of the cleverest and kindest creatures in the whole of Melas, and definitely in Dralfynia." We all looked at him admiringly. Clyde deafened us with an almighty paaarp and we all quickly took several steps away because we knew what would start to waft toward our nostrils if we didn't.

"Well, there's at least one piece of good news," Olive said suddenly. "I asked my Dad not to build anything on Clyde's field and he agreed."

"That was nice of you," I said reluctantly. It would have been terrible if Clyde's home had suddenly been turned into a sewage works, though it might have smelled a bit nicer. I sighed. We had gotten nowhere and it was time to go home.

"At least it's Friday tomorrow," I said. "Only one more day till the weekend and maybe we can figure something out then. In the meantime, we should just keep with crowds of people and avoid Witchy Wu as best we can."

"But then," Olive said, "it's your brother's birthday party, remember?" We all looked at each other. That was true. How could we have forgotten? That was when the Beast and Witchy Wu were planning to steal Ruggy. Olive's words finally sparked my brain into working.

"Guys, I've just had a brilliant idea," I said excitedly. The beginnings of a plan were starting for form. Maybe there was a way out of this after all. Yes, I could definitely see a way out of this mess. "I think you guys should come to the party," I told Persis and Olive. "As long as he gets a gift, Rory won't care who comes." I babbled on, not stopping for breath in case they tried to interrupt and say something like, "Never in a million-billion years would we go to an eight-year-old boy's birthday party full of other eight-year-old boys, thanks." After I had outlined my plan, they both looked at each other, shrugged and agreed to come along. Besides, I definitely needed some moral support to cope with one of Rory's parties.

We spent Friday at school squashing into the gaps between the lockers to hide, walking very closely behind people who were taller than us, or scuttling along as low as we could below window level. By cutting Home Room again, and cookery too, we managed to avoid Witchy Wu. We were geniuses.

That evening, while I was in the kitchen at home helping Bridget make one of her infamous gray, gloopy stews I felt pretty happy with myself. I had figured out a plan which meant that not only would Ruggy be safe, but that we would also capture Witchy Wu in the act of trying to steal something from a kid's bedroom. It was a perfect plan and I was very proud of it. It was simple: Olive and Persis would hide in Rory's bedroom while he, his friends and the adults all went over to the park. I'd find an excuse to sneak back and join them. When Witchy Wu arrived, we three would record her on our phones and then tell the police and the school. She'd be locked up and we'd be safe again.

Plus, Uncle Don was sure to come to Rory's party. He never missed either of our birthdays. I was still feeling happy when I went to answer the phone as it rang, leaving Bridget in the kitchen stirring and looking anxiously at her recipe book.

"Summers' residence," I said cheerfully.

"Hello Sabrina," a man's voice replied.

Oh dear. This was not going to be good. I recognized that voice immediately.

"This is Principal McPhail. Is your father home? I understand that you and two other girls have been skipping school."

CHAPTER
6

I couldn't believe that Witchy Wu had told on us to Principal McPhail. How low could she sink? Dad was not happy with me and after I texted Olive and Persis, I found that their parents were not happy either.

As a punishment we had been given detention on Monday after school and Ms. Wu would be "looking after" us. And while we were there, we had to give her letters of apology that we were supposed to write during the weekend. I didn't know about the other two, but there was no way I was writing an apology letter. There were two reasons for that: first up, she was a mean witch who only recently had wanted to fatten us and eat us; and second, she would have been arrested already if my fantastic plan worked.

On Saturday morning, we were all woken up nice and early by Rory "accidentally" dropping things loudly on the ground and then "accidentally" slamming doors. Groaning, I rolled out of bed and helped make pancakes for breakfast, which had become a new Summers' family tradition since Bridget had joined us. Rory was so excited that he became a chaotic red-headed whirlwind on two little legs, spinning around the house and causing destruction. After he had shoveled four pancakes into his mouth without bothering to chew, he opened his presents and scattered paper and boxes around the whole house. Then he ran to the field to say 'hi' to Clyde, ignoring Dad's shouts to put on a rain jacket. He returned half an hour later covered in mud, with his hair plastered to his head.

"I don't think meeting your friends at the park is a good idea," said Dad, as he tucked Rory under his arm and headed for the shower.

"BUT I WANT TO GO TO THE PARK AND PLAY!" was Rory's ear-splitting reply.

"But it's raining and it's not going to ease up," said Dad. "You'll all be soaked and catch colds."

"BUT I WANT TO CATCH A COLD SO I DON'T HAVE TO GO TO SCHOOL ON MONDAY," said Rory, wriggling in Dad's grip. I gave him points for honesty, and I agreed with him that his party should go ahead but not for the same reasons. I needed an apparently empty house for when Witchy Wu arrived to try to steal Ruggy.

"Dad, I think it's kind of late notice to contact all those parents," I interrupted. "What happens if you manage to get some of them and they come here, but the others still go to the park?" Dad gave a shrug, bouncing Rory up and down on his hip.

"OK," he said. "You can go to the park as long as you have a proper shower, soap and everything, and we don't stay there too long."

I rubbed my hands. My plan was working out. I'd go along pretending to be the supportive big sister as if I wanted to help supervise all the kids before they came back here for take-out pizzas, but I planned to fake a headache and come home earlier.

I had planned to sneak Persis and Olive in once everyone had left but we were late and they were early so I had no choice but to introduce them to Dad and Bridget. They were pretty surprised to see any friends of mine on a day like today. Usually my friends run for the farthest hills they can find if Rory is having a party. I explained that they were friends with Rory as well as with me.

"Really?" said Dad and Bridget together. They obviously didn't believe me. I improvised. "Well, they both want to be elementary school teachers when they grow up and I thought this might be a real test for them."

Persis and Olive put down their presents and offered to clean up all Rory's mess while the rest of us went to the park. Dad was pleased and said thanks, but Bridget drew me to one side.

"Sabrina," she said. Uh oh. "Sabrina" meant that she was serious; I usually got called "Brina". I don't think she was convinced that two twelve-year-old girls wanted to hang out at a boy's eighth birthday party. "Sabrina, is something going on that I should know about?" The answer to that question was yes.

"No," I said, avoiding her eyes. She didn't say anything else, but I'm sure she believed me.

Probably.

She stared at Olive, who dipped her head and carried an armful of wrapping paper to the kitchen. She was likely thinking that Olive looked a lot a girl dressed as Cinderella she had recently met in Dralfynia.

"Hmm," said Bridget.

I guess she didn't believe me after all but Bridget had a party to run and no time to worry about us right now.

As she, Dad and Rory headed out the door, I yelled that I would catch them up. Then I quickly showed Persis and Olive where to hide, and hurried out into the rain and joined my family. I pulled my hood up and tried to avoid the puddles. Rory jumped into them with both feet, doing his best to splash me.

His friends met us there and, after wasting a few minutes of my life watching a group of boys scream and yell and throw stuff, I collected up an armful of his gifts. I turned to my dad.

"Hey, I've got a bit of a headache. Shall I take these presents home with me and have a rest before you all come back?" He nodded. His attention was focused on a game the boys were playing. It wasn't subtle. Whenever anyone came near them, they tried to drench them by pulling down on tree branches and then letting go suddenly so that the other boy was soaked by a shower of raindrops.

I ran home as fast as I could, and a few minutes later I dripped back into the house and shook myself like a dog. I dumped Rory's presents on the floor then I stood very still and listened. I couldn't hear a thing. Great, I was in time. Olive and Persis must already be in position, hiding in Rory's bedroom. I started to climb the stairs to go and join them.

From above me I heard a creak. That must be Persis, I thought to myself. She can never keep still. I took another step and then there was another creak. I opened my mouth to shush Persis but a little voice inside my head told me to keep quiet. I don't usually listen to any kind of voice that tells me to keep quiet, but today the voice was very insistent.

Instead of calling to Persis, I took a step backward, then another. I was as quiet as a mouse wearing shoes made from cotton wool. I reached the bottom of the stairs and crept over to the living room door. I stood there, out of sight, and waited.

Then the creaking got louder and more regular. Someone was coming toward the stairs that led right to me and they were running.

CHAPTER 7

I dropped down to a crouch and as quietly as I could I scuttled back to the staircase and slipped into the gap between it and the wall. I was pressed into the narrow space where Rory usually dumped his bike and sports equipment and it was full of his junk. Whoever was up there had crossed the landing and was starting to hurry down the stairs, not even bothering to be quiet. Their noise covered the sounds I made when I moved. I looked up and peered between the wooden stairs to the hand rail. Those black shoes with buckles again! It was Witchy Wu, and her feet were almost level with my nose. For every step she took there was a bumping sound behind her.

"Come on, you annoying lump of woven wool! Stop being a naughty boy," she said.

I looked higher up. She was dragging poor Ruggy along behind her. He was all rolled up and tied in the middle with a piece of string. He was being bashed against each step but he fought back. He wriggled and bucked with all his might. She stopped and stooped. I was terrified she would see me but all her attention was on Ruggy as she picked him up. Ruggy had the same moves as Rory had when he was two years old and having a tantrum. He kicked out with one end and while she grappled with that he reared up and lashed out with the other end, knocking her hard on the back.

Good old Ruggy. But something had obviously gone wrong. For some reason she had arrived early and Persis and Olive hadn't managed to stop her.

I didn't have time to think; I only had time to act.

As Ruggy continued to fight back, I carefully reached behind me, hoping my hands would make contact with something useful. My fingers closed on a smooth cylinder-shaped object. I gripped it hard and then gently lifted it out. It was a softball bat. Perfect. I slid it carefully between the wooden bars so that it went across the stairs at ankle level, closed my eyes and yelled out.

"Hey, Witchy Wu—can't you even steal an old rug properly?"

I braced my feet firmly on the floor and, just as I had hoped, she started to run down the stairs. I felt the pressure against the bat as Witchy Wu's ankles made contact. I struggled to hold on to the handle as the pressure increased, but finally she toppled forward. I kept my eyes closed as I heard a screech and a sickening thud as she fell heavily and landed hard on the wooden floor of our hallway.

I leaped out and jumped onto Witchy Wu's back as she lay sprawled on the floor, shrieking at the top of my voice, "That's not yours; give it back! Give it back!" I was stuck onto her like a very tight backpack, and she started to twist and turn to get me off. "Persis! Olive! A little help here!" I yelled.

Witchy Wu dropped Ruggy on the floor. Now that her arms were free, she could twist around so she tried to roll on top of me and squash me like a bug. From the corner of my eye I spotted Ruggy. He started to ripple the way a snake does when it moves, and reared up as if he was going to strike her again, but she flung out one of her hands and hissed a spell at him.

"This is the rug that I desire, but first it will be consumed with fire." I whacked at her arm just in time. A flash exploded from her hand but instead of landing on Ruggy it zoomed harmlessly to the ceiling, leaving a sooty patch on the clean white paint. I would deal with that later, I decided.

Suddenly we heard car doors slamming and voices from outside.

Witchy Wu snarled at me and slashed out with her nails, but I arched backward in time. She jumped to her feet and limped to the back of the house. I had hurt her leg when I tripped her down the stairs. I reached for Ruggy hoping to run and hide upstairs, but it was too late: just as I heard the backdoor slam closed, the front door opened—and there on the doorstep stood several people, staring at me.

I was spread across the hallway floor like a starfish, clutching a rolled-up rug in one hand. My hair was a mess, I was bright red and I was covered in dust. Seriously, we had to make more effort to vacuum this house—I'd have to have a word with Bridget.

"Why is my softball bat on the stairs, and why is there a big dent in it?" Rory asked. Luckily, I didn't even have to say anything—everyone just assumed it was Rory's fault.

"Oh Rory, you've left your stuff on the stairs again," Bridget said crossly. "And now look, poor Brina's fallen down stairs because of it." It was brilliant. I couldn't have thought of a better excuse myself.

The next thing I knew I was being scooped up by Uncle Don, who had arrived with everyone else, and fussed over and checked for injuries by Dad and Bridget.

"I'm OK, honestly," I said, pulling away. I hate being made a fuss of and I needed to get up to Rory's room to find out what had happened to Olive and Persis. They should have come to see what all the noise was by now.

Rory was the only one who didn't join in the chaos. He stood on the edge of the crowd, his eyes narrowed. He glared first at me, then at

Ruggy, then at me. At some point I was going to have to tell him that the terrifying witch who wanted to eat him had just gate-crashed his eighth birthday party. Oh, and I should probably apologize for denting his bat and letting him take the blame, but that could wait.

CHAPTER
8

While everyone else headed into the den for movies, pizza and ice cream, I scooped poor Ruggy up and snuck up to Rory's bedroom. I was starting to worry about Olive and Persis.

I opened the door and was hit by the usual smell of sweaty socks, half-eaten sandwiches that had had the middles licked out, and paint for his models. This time it was even worse than normal. It also smelled like armpits. I pinched my nose closed with my fingers and walked in. It wasn't just the smell that was shocking—the whole room was also filled with a green glow. My mouth dropped open as I stood and stared about me, and I let go of my nose. As I looked around, the glow began to fade. I yawned hugely. My eyelids started to droop. This was no time to feel sleepy. Maybe it was delayed shock after fighting Witchy Wu; I had read that people felt tired after doing brave and scary things. I shook my head to get rid of the sleepy feeling and went to the closet door to see if Persis was hidden in there as planned.

I yawned again and my knees began to give way. I wanted nothing more than to lie down on Rory's messy bed and close my eyes. A little nap would be wonderful right now.

I didn't make it to the closet. I sat on the edge of the bed and heard a little squeak. Oh that's right, I'd told Olive to hide underneath it, I remembered. Strange, she must be having a nap too.

Eventually my brain began to pester me loudly enough to take notice of what it was thinking. I had to ignore my super-relaxed and very comfortable body, nestling amongst the blankets. My brain said that Witchy Wu must have cast a sleeping spell—and that it was still working.

Then there was a short argument between my brain and my body which my brain only just won. My legs felt very heavy, but I forced them to move and dragged myself back to the hallway outside the bedrooms. I took some breaths of clean air in and forced the old air out. Straight away I began to feel better. I filled my lungs as deeply as I could with the clean air and went back into Rory's bedroom; I hurried across to his windows and threw them open as wide as I could then let out my breath with a whoosh. I leaned half out and half in for a few minutes panting and watching the green glow stream out of the window. As I watched, it drifted gently to the ground and started to dissolve but not before I saw three birds fall asleep on their branch, next door's dog snuggle down in his yard and the paper boy suddenly curl up under a bush and begin to snore.

I heard a scrabbling noise from behind me and turned back around. Olive was crawling out from underneath Rory's bed. She stretched her arms out and yawned widely. There were dust bunnies stuck to her hair and clothes. I went and opened the closet. Somehow Persis had managed to sleep comfortably standing up, draped over coat hangers. She snored gently.

I sighed. They were my friends, even Olive, but sometimes a girl just has to do a job herself to get it done properly.

CHAPTER 9

O live and Persis felt great after their long sleep and they joined in with the party games, but later on, while Persis jogged back home clutching a piece of birthday cake, Olive hesitated on the sidewalk in front of the Summers' house.

She knew that Sabrina wouldn't want her talking to Bridget, but she also knew that they were in a lot of trouble and they needed some help and advice. As far as Olive could figure, Bridget was the only person that they could turn to. She looked down at the piece of birthday cake that Sabrina had pressed into her hand when she let her and Persis out of the house. It was sticky and a bit squashed but it had been a very kind and generous thing for Sabrina to do: she had made Olive feel as important to her as Persis was.

She took a bite of the cake. Yummy. A bit warm but definitely yummy. Before she knew it, she had eaten it all, licked her fingers and had remained staring at Sabrina's house instead of heading home. It was getting dark as evening approached and still she stood on the sidewalk trying to decide what to do.

She heard a rustling in the shrubs nearby and whirled around, suddenly frightened. If she wasn't going to go talk to Bridget she should go home before it got too late. A figure rose, picked up a bike and a satchel full of newspapers and let out a huge yawn. The paper boy scratched his tummy, looked around him as if he was a little surprised to find that he had been sleeping in someone's garden, climbed onto his bike and slowly pedaled away.

Olive let out a breath of relief—then jumped almost out of her socks when a hand fell on her shoulder. She spun around, remembering that they had no idea where Witchy Wu had gone after she ran from the house.

Instead, Bridget stood there, looking down at her. She got straight to the point. "What's going on, Olive?" she asked. Olive cleared her throat nervously several times while Bridget waited silently. Stumbling over her words, and with lots of pauses while she tried to remember everything that had happened, Olive told her. As Olive explained, Bridget's eyebrows climbed higher and higher up her forehead, and her mouth opened wider and wider. "I tried to get Sabrina and Persis to come talk to you, but … you know," Olive finished with a shrug of her shoulders.

Bridget nodded. "Yes, I know." She paused for a minute as she tried to make sense of Olive's story. "So, the problems we have are …" she began, holding up her hand in a fist and unfolding a finger for each problem she described. "Number one: my old friend Wu Ling has made the trip to Melas. She wouldn't have done something like that by herself; she's a follower of the Beast so my guess is that he instructed her to come here." She gave a sigh. "That's not good news. OK, number two: she wants the magic rug and she's already been to your school and this house to get it. It sounds like she won't stop until she does. Number three: the Beast himself must be nearby too." Bridget grimaced. She looked very unhappy. "Those compact-mirror phones don't work over a long distance, you see," she explained. "Now, I wonder," she mused. Her eyebrows came back down her forehead and bunched up instead as she thought about the Beast with Eight Fingers for a moment. She puffed out a breath and unfolded another finger. "And number four: Sabrina doesn't trust me since she discovered that I am a witch, so we can't tell her that we've talked." She looked at Olive. "Does that about cover it all?"

Olive nodded miserably. When Bridget put it all together, it sounded impossible. There was no way out. They could just give Ruggy to Witchy Wu and hope for the best, she supposed. But that did not guarantee that they would be left alone. And what would happen to the people of Dralfynia? She thought about Aidan and his cute dimples, Russell the talking tree, and the villagers and townspeople they had met there.

Bridget stood pulling her bottom lip out with her finger and thumb and then letting it go again. Each time she did so, it made a little plopping sound. She was clearly in deep thought. Then she snapped her fingers together making Olive jump. "OK, there's only one way out of this," she said. "You kids have to go back to Dralfynia—and you have to take Ruggy with you."

CHAPTER 10

Bridget ignored Olive's protests about never, ever wanting to return to somewhere that had no cell phone coverage, no flushing toilets and no Internet access. Instead, she started to work out the practicalities. She gave a quick nod. Yes, she could make a short-acting potion that would send them back to Dralfynia, and it was going to be up to Olive to persuade them to take it.

"There's no point in me trying to get Sabrina to take a potion," Bridget explained. "She'll never do it if she knows I'm involved." Olive nodded unhappily. There was slightly more chance of Sabrina taking something that Olive offered her, but not much. She complained and argued, but in the end, there had been no real point in disagreeing with Bridget. She had come this far to ask for help and she would just have to say "yes" to whatever plan Bridget thought up.

Having seen Olive safely home and arranged to give her the completed potion later, Bridget returned to her kitchen. The rest of her family were already in bed. As midnight fell across Melas, she stood over her stove, murmuring spells that she read out from a tatty, old book. The book was labeled "Healthy Recipes with Brussels Sprouts" so she knew no one would ever pick it up, and her secret charms were well-hidden within its pages. As she spoke, she waved her hands over a pot of a clear, bubbling liquid. It sent occasional vivid, pink sparks into the air and it smelled like dead flies, which were, in fact, one of the ingredients—there was a reason Bridget didn't vacuum quite as thoroughly as she could have. As she worked, Bridget let her mind wander back and back, away and away, until she was only two years older than Sabrina and her friends were now, and she was still living in Dralfynia. She thought about an old friendship, and a single act that had shaped both her life and that of her friend.

"Miss Wu? Miss Bishop? Please stop giggling at the back of class and pay attention." The teacher telling them off just made Ling and Bridget giggle even more. Even if they had detention at the end of the day, they didn't mind because they would be together. They were the two top student witches in their year and they knew they could catch up on any missed work easily.

After three years at witch school, Ling and Bridget had been through a lot together. Bridget had been the first person to stick up for Ling when some of the other kids had tried to bully her. They picked on her just because her family had moved to Dralfynia from a different land, so her traditions and clothes were not the same. Ling had repaid the kindness by helping Bridget with broom-riding lessons after seeing that she kept falling off.

They had quickly become SDBFs (or super-duper best friends) and they knew that nothing would ever come between them. They practiced spells together and showed each other the new potions and magic spells they invented. After lights out in the dormitory where all the student witches slept, Ling and Bridget would whisper their dreams and secrets to each other. They shared a goal. After they left school, they would live in a house in a forest. It would be the most delicious gingerbread cottage ever baked. They would trade enchantments and potions with the villagers in exchange for other goods, and they would grow herbs and vegetables. Yes, the future looked not just rosy, but yummy, cotton-candy pink.

But something did come between them. Something that was supposed to be good. It wasn't new friends who separated them; it wasn't even a boy that they quarreled over. It was a competition. A silly competition to win the Golden Broom trophy for the best young witch.

It was a fabulous prize, mind you. The winner would become famous and would live in the Royal Castle in Timaru. She would have a life of luxury and be able to travel between lands. Future witches would study the winner's work and she would be admired wherever she went. Still, it was just a contest; it shouldn't have mattered who won. It should not have destroyed a friendship.

But it did. The contest turned friend against friend, and brothers and sisters against each other right across the school. To her own surprise, Bridget was desperate to win. She had never won anything in her life. She always came last in races and her older brothers and sisters had teased her, telling her she was slow and clumsy. Now, when Bridget went to bed at night, she turned her back on Ling and kept her dreams to herself. She imagined herself being friends with royalty, wearing the finest robes, going to visit schools and being mobbed by her fans. For the first time ever, her family would be jealous of her. No one would laugh at her or tease her again. The longer the competition went on, the more secretive Bridget became. She spent all her time studying and practicing magic. She avoided Ling and lied about where she had been and what she had been doing.

Left on her own, Ling also began to study hard. By the final day of the contest, both girls were in equal first place. The decision rested on who could invent the best sleeping spell.

They called the contestants up in alphabetical order so Bridget climbed the steps to the stage first and stood in front of the whole school and all the parents and families of the students. Her hands shook from nerves as she pounded herbs in her cauldron and added other ingredients. She talked about what she was doing in a trembling voice and answered the judges' questions haltingly. When she had finished, a green glow came from the cauldron. The volunteer who had offered to test the spell snoozed peacefully, lying on a bench in the middle of the stage. Not even the loud cheering of the other students was enough to wake him up. Bridget looked over at the judges. They were nodding, impressed with what they had seen. She did not dare to look into the audience. She knew who she would see there and she could guess what she would be thinking.

Surely nothing could beat Bridget's spell. An excited buzz went around the room and people began talking about Bridget as the out-right winner. Sitting in the audience, waiting for her turn, Ling clenched her fists, bunching up the skirt of her silk gown. She had just watched Bridget demonstrate her spell, the one that she, Wu Ling, had perfected several weeks earlier, long before the competition began. She had proudly shared it with Bridget. Bridget had been happy for her and had congratulated her. She had said that people who didn't sleep well would be grateful for the new spell. Now, Ling shook her head in disbelief. There was no doubt in her mind that Bridget had betrayed her and stolen her spell so that she could win the Golden Broom.

As she sat there, a single tear rolled down Ling's pale cheek. It landed with a splash on the back of her hands. She wept a single tear for her friend's disloyalty—she wept it because she knew she had lost her SDBF and she wept for the happy future she would never now have. But the other witches thought she was jealous.

"Look! That witch has shed a tear," someone gasped. A hiss skittered around the room as all the parents, teachers and student witches stared at Ling. She looked down at her tear. It glistened like a jewel. Then, with a sudden movement, she rubbed it away. So what if witches can only shed three tears before they die? So what if she could only ever shed two more tears in her life? She didn't care. She felt the pain in her heart as sharply as if Bridget had stabbed her there with a knife. She got to her feet and stumbled from the room. She didn't look at anyone else as she went. She especially didn't look at Bridget as she stood on the stage, holding the solid gold trophy in her hands.

CHAPTER
11

Twenty years on and Bridget's hands trembled again as she poured her potion into an old-fashioned glass bottle with a cork. She blinked as hard as she could to chase away her own tear. She could not afford to waste one on regret. A single moment of weakness had changed both Wu Ling and Bridget Bishop herself.

The trophy had felt like a poisonous snake in her hands as soon as it was handed to her. She had run through the school calling Ling's name, looking for her friend so that she could try to apologize and explain. She had decided to give the trophy to Ling. She deserved it more than Bridget; she had always been the better witch. Bridget was going to tell Ling she would tell the truth and give the trophy to her.

But Ling had gone. She had walked out of the school and she had never once looked back.

Bridget had wanted to put things right but with Ling missing she had no reason to admit what she had done and she was too ashamed to speak up. She didn't want everyone to know that she had stolen the spell.

And so the years had passed. Bridget learned that Ling had gone to the forest and her bitterness had poisoned the earth so that it became

Scary Forest. She had tried to counter her bitterness with more and more sweet things, but still it had filled her heart. She became known as Witchy Wu, the witch who hated to see happy children. When she found that mothers were using her to frighten children into being good and staying at home, she had been pleased. She told people that she would fatten up their children and eat them if they came to her home, which certainly made sure that she was left in peace.

For her part, Bridget turned her back on her dreams. Instead of a life of fame and riches, Bridget had chosen to live quietly in Tylwyth Teg, keeping out of the spotlight as much as possible. She spent her life giving her time, love and skills to others, hoping it would stop the guilt she felt. Eventually she realized that her kindness helped other people and she enjoyed how that made her feel. She knew that she would never betray a friend again nor take credit for someone else's work. The guilt faded, and was replaced by a longing to make Wu Ling feel as calm and happy as she did.

Over time, Witchy Wu and Bridget had found themselves on opposite sides of matters in Dralfynia. As the Beast's power spread, Bridget had fought to protect the people and creatures who were loyal to his missing sister. But Witchy Wu had fought viciously and victoriously on the side of the Beast. She had been happy to finally beat Bridget by harming those she cared about.

When Duchess Yvonne had visited Bridget and asked her to come to this strange land full of noise and dirt and frightening technology, Bridget had agreed. Anything to stop the cruel Beast taking over their land. Although she hadn't been able to find poor Princess Heidi, she had found something else. She had found a husband and a family.

She held up the old glass bottle to the light, checking it was clean and not cracked. As she poured some of the potion into it, her mind whirled. She hoped she was doing the right thing. Yes, Melas was dangerous now that Witchy Wu had come, that was for sure. But would Dralfynia be even more perilous for Sabrina and the others? She decided they would need some help. She decided to visit Clyde.

CHAPTER
12

U ncle Don stayed for the weekend and spent the time taking Rory and me out to the mall and the movies, even though I was technically grounded for getting detention. Didn't I tell you he was cool? On the other hand, Bridget was asking me a whole lot of questions about why I didn't like the new teacher and what did she look like. Dad was cross that I had been skipping class and wouldn't give him a reason. But what could I say? I didn't want to tell lies to my dad, and I sure couldn't tell him the truth, so I just said "I don't know." In fact, he was so cross that I was given extra chores, and because Rory was the "birthday boy", I got to clean his room.

Surprisingly, that turned out to be quite fun. As I had seen when he was escaping from Witchy Wu, Ruggy still had his magic in him. When I used the vacuum cleaner on him, it tickled him and he rolled from side to side as if he was giggling. When I stopped, he inched his way back toward me as if he was asking for more.

"Come on," I said. I was using the same voice that people use when they are playing with puppies. "C'mon Ruggy. Good boy!"

"Ahem," I heard from behind me. I wheeled around, blushing. Uncle

Don stood there grinning. "Talking to furniture?" he asked. I blushed even redder. He came into Rory's room and looked down at Ruggy, who was thankfully pretending to be, well, a rug. He gave a little whistle and then picked up Ruggy, holding him up to the light to get a better view. "Rugs like this are quite valuable," he told me, admiring the pattern and the rich colors. "Where did Rory get it?"

"Ummmmmm, I'm not sure; I think maybe he found it in a dumpster," I said, hoping that he wouldn't be able to tell I was not quite telling the truth.

"Huh," said Uncle Don. "Well, he needs to take care of it. I could look after it for him. In fact, I could sell it for quite a lot of money and put it into his savings account."

Sell Ruggy? SELL Ruggy? My mouth opened and closed like a fish, while I tried to think of something to say.

"Rory's very fond of that rug; it's not for sale." Bridget spoke calmly, but she made us both jump.

"I see," said Uncle Don. He handed Ruggy back to me, telling me again that it was a very special rug and that we should look after it. I smiled to myself. If only he knew just how special Ruggy was.

The weekend flew past way too quickly. One minute Dad was getting the call from Principal McPhail, the next I was being bundled into the car with him and Bridget and taken to school to make sure I got to my first class, which was, of course, Home Room.

The butterflies in my tummy were jumping up and down, doing flips and headstands, and generally going crazy. My mouth was dry with nerves. I was even relieved to have Bridget with me. If anything went wrong, at least I knew she was a witch and would surely help me. As we pulled into the car park, I looked around to see who was already there. I recognized Persis' and Olive's parents' cars. I almost expected to see a broomstick parked in with the pushbikes and scooters but I was disappointed. I sighed and got out of the car as slowly as I possibly could.

"Sabrina, hurry up," Dad said. "You need to just get this over with and move on, OK? You'll write an apology letter, do detention after school and that will be that. What could go wrong?"

What indeed?

CHAPTER 13

And so my second strange saga—and my second journey to Dralfynia—began in the girls' bathroom at school. Here's how it happened.

Firstly: on Sunday evening Olive texted me to say that she had a great idea, but needed to explain it face-to-face, and that Rory should take Ruggy to school for show-and-tell instead of leaving him at home.

Secondly: Olive, Persis and I stomped into the classroom, and in front of Principal McPhail and the whole class we muttered, "Sorry for skipping your lessons, Ms. Wu."

Thirdly: Olive spent the whole day being super-mysterious and saying that everything would be revealed during detention. I sure hoped so—if Witchy Wu was ever going to make a move on us, it would be then. The school would be empty and we would be at her mercy. Unless we skipped detention, that is—but then, skipping detention for skipping class was really asking for trouble.

Fourthly: during one of our breaks, we sneaked across to the elementary school, which joins onto our middle school. Olive wanted to see Rory and put the beginnings of her plan into action.

We weren't really supposed to go to the elementary school so we darted across the shared yard, hiding behind pillars and trash cans like spies. I caught Persis' eye. She was having fun, I could tell, especially when she suddenly dropped down, did an unnecessary and dramatic forward roll, and popped up again with just her head showing over the top of a trash can.

We eventually arrived outside Rory's classroom and crowded around to look through the window that was cut into the door. They were still having lessons—their break was a few minutes after ours to avoid the yard getting too crowded.

The windows had been put in a couple of years earlier, around the same time Rory had transferred to the school. They were there so that if anything bad happened in the classroom, or there was some kind of emergency, the other teachers could look inside and see what was going on.

Coincidence? I don't think so.

"What's he doing?" asked Olive. As we watched the rest of the children reading from books on their desk, we saw that Rory had a clear piece of plastic over his book. It was tinted orange. Also, his book was much larger, and the font was bigger.

"He's dyslexic," I explained, seeing Olive's expression. "It was terrible at his last school. The teachers didn't help him much and he thought that he was just dumb. All he needed was someone to explain to him that his brain just works a bit differently, and show him ways to deal with it." I shook my head, still angry at the way Rory had been treated. "His new teacher, Mr. Rees-Owen, has been great," I said. "Now Rory thinks that being dyslexic rocks, because so many famous people are dyslexic and he's sure he'll be a superstar when he grows up. Plus," I added, "his behavior is much better now he isn't so frustrated."

Boy, did I speak too soon.

Rory was sitting near his friends Nathan and Heath. Nathan stood up to walk behind Rory's desk so he could go see the teacher. As soon as he tried to get past, Rory pushed his seat back, blocking Nathan's route. When Nathan went to turn back, Rory shuffled his feet so that he moved his seat back under his desk. Then Nathan went to walk past Rory again. Quickly, Rory pushed with his feet and his chair moved backward so he was in Nathan's way again. Nathan sighed and took a much longer route to the front of the class, leaving Rory innocently reading his book as if nothing had happened.

Then Heath held out his hand. He seemed to be asking to borrow a pencil. Rory picked up one of his spare pencils and offered it to Heath. As Heath reached to take it, Rory pulled it back again. After five times, Heath lost his patience and yanked the pencil from Rory's closed fist. Unbelievably, Rory looked offended, and then he grinned broadly.

This was fascinating. Embarrassing but fascinating. We couldn't stop watching. Over the next five minutes we saw my little brother kick his backpack into the walkway to try and trip one of the little girls in his class; then he got up and wandered around the classroom reading over the shoulders of other kids and making comments; finally, he decided to pack up five minutes before the bell went and sat there, arms crossed, coat on, staring at the wall.

"Oh Sabrina," Olive said softly. "You poor, poor thing." I didn't reply. What could I say? She was right.

Finally the bell went. We stepped out of the way. Little kids leaving class can be terrifying. Rory got to the door first and deliberately stood in everyone's way for a few seconds before sniggering and popping into the corridor like a cork.

The shocked expression on his face when he saw the three of us and realized we had been watching him was priceless.

I grabbed his arm and pulled him along in the opposite direction from everyone else. We needed a few minutes for the crowds to disappear.

"What's going on?" asked Rory, looking as guilty as a dog who just ate your lunch when your back was turned.

"We have a problem," I said.

"It wasn't my fault," he replied. It was his standard answer to most things, usually not true, so I ignored him.

"It's Witchy Wu," I said. "Remember her?" He nodded. "She's here, in Melas. She's our new Home Room teacher."

It took him a little while to understand what I had told him. Then his mouth dropped right open and his eyes bugged. "That's bad," he said.

"It's OK," said Olive, "I have a plan."

CHAPTER
14

nd finally, right when we were shuffling into detention as Principal McPhail and Witchy Wu (her black eye and her green eye sparkling with excitement) watched us, Olive's plan sparked into action.

"Come in, girls," Witchy Wu said, hopping around and rubbing her hands in glee. "Take a seat. We have such a lot to 'discuss', don't we?" She hooked her fingers as she said the word 'discuss' to let us know that we probably wouldn't be doing a lot of talking; we'd probably be having magic done to us instead. The principal gave us all a nod. He had on the disappointed expression on that he wore when us kids had let him down in some way. He raised a hand of support to Witchy Wu then strode away down the corridor. Now that he knew we had turned up, he was leaving us to be dealt with by her.

"So Miss Clever Cookie," I whispered to Olive as we hesitated in the doorway, "what next?"

"Shush," she said to me. "Just wait and follow my lead." I frowned but I couldn't stand there forever, so I slowly went into the classroom and sat at a desk as close to the door as I could. Persis and Olive sat next to me. Witchy Wu slammed the door closed and gave an evil witchy laugh. We put our hands over our ears. It was pretty shrill. I think maybe a pane of glass cracked too.

She walked over to us, put her hands on her hips and tapped her foot. She looked at us one by one, as if she was sizing us up to see which of us would taste better.

"The Beast himself will be here to deal with you very soon, girls," she announced. We all did the cold, runny blood thing again. She clapped her hands with delight at our gasps of shock.

The Beast with Eight Fingers? In Melas? In our school?

Gulp.

From behind us there was a slow scratching on the window that fronted onto the school yard. Persis and I tensed where we sat. Was that him? The scratching came again, setting our teeth tingling in our mouths.

It obviously annoyed Witchy Wu too because she left us and strode to the window. She rapped on it with her knuckles. Two heads with dark brown hair and mischievous brown eyes popped up, looked at her, then popped down again. Behind them, I thought I caught a glimpse of a horse in our school yard, but I blinked and it was gone. I shook my head and heard a sound from the other side of the room. I turned to look and another head with red hair and mischievous blue eyes popped up in the window cut into the door to the classroom. Rory was there, gesturing for us to go and join him. Olive half-rose but saw that Witchy Wu was coming back over. She slid down into her seat again. The scraping returned and this time I recognized Nathan and Heath as they started to throw small pebbles and sticks at the window. Witchy Wu tried to ignore them, but I could see by the way her jaw twitched and her teeth clenched that they were really annoying her.

She stomped over to the window and started banging on it with her fist, shouting at Rory's two friends to go away. At the same time, Olive jumped up and ran for the door. For a whole second, Persis and I stared at each other, then leaped up too, and ran as fast as if a terrifying witch was right behind us.

We skidded into the corridor where Rory stood. As soon as we were out, he slammed the door and turned a key in the lock. Witchy Wu appeared in the window and glared at us, then she began rattling the handle and screeching at us.

I started to ask Rory where he had gotten a master key for Melas Middle School, but realized that I didn't really want to know. That way, if any grown up asked me, I could tell the truth.

"Hurry up!" yelled Olive as she ran along the corridor. She was headed for the girls' bathroom again. I started to argue as I ran.

"Shouldn't we be getting out of school, not going even deeper into the building?" I panted. I risked a glance back at Witchy Wu. She was talking to someone on her compact-mirror phone. Uh-oh. If the Beast was nearby, he'd be coming to rescue her and no doubt get us too. And because Rory was dragging Ruggy with him, if he caught us then there was no reason for him to keep us alive. I had no choice. I had to have faith that Olive really did have a plan. I started to run faster.

CHAPTER 15

"And then what? Oh yuk, this tastes gross." I began my sentence in the girls' bathroom in what I was starting to think of as "our cubicle". I ended my sentence in a very smelly, wooden room with straw on the floor, and a long plank with holes cut in it for people to sit on and—well, never mind, you can guess what for.

Oh yes, and in between I had been spun around and around and upside down as a strange fog swirled around me. It seared my eyes and nose and throat, taking my breath away for a few seconds, and it scratched against my skin. It had felt like being in a tumble-drier wearing an outfit made from sandpaper but I didn't feel fluffed up and warm. In fact, I felt chilly.

I gave a little shiver then stared at Olive with my meanest gaze.

"What.

Exactly.

Was.

That.

All.

About?" I demanded, separating each word significantly so she would know how mad I was.

Except that I realized I wasn't staring at Olive anymore. I was staring at a girl who looked like Olive, but who had yellow hair in braids that flicked up at the ends like curly fries. She wore a blue-and-white checked dress with a little white apron trimmed with lace, little white ankle socks and a lapel pin that read 'I heart porridge.' My stomach dropped down a couple of inches and I stopped speaking. I closed my eyes. I didn't want to see anymore. Although I couldn't see her, I could still hear the sound of Olive trying to dry retch behind her fingers in a ladylike way. I squeezed my eyes shut harder, and stuck a finger in each ear.

Oh no. No-no-no-no-no.

Not again.

Olive had dragged us into the bathroom, dripped some icky stuff onto our tongues and told us to hold tight. Then had come the tumble-drier thing and then, when I looked at Olive, she had become Goldilocks.

She had tricked me. It all meant one thing and I didn't want to think about it. I started to do some math problems in my head to make myself think of something else instead.

"What's 11 x 7?" I asked myself.

"Dralfynia," I answered myself. I sighed. I couldn't hide from the truth even though I really, really wanted to. Somehow Olive had helped us escape from Witchy Wu and the Beast with Eight Fingers by bringing us to the place where all the trouble had started. We were back in Dralfynia.

After I had sighed, I groaned a little as well. If we were in Dralfynia and Olive was Goldilocks, who was I? Last time I had been Rapunzel, she had been Cinderella, Persis had been Little Red Riding Hood and Rory had been Ali Baba. I put my hand carefully onto my hair. When I had been Rapunzel it had been a huge mass that had given me a stiff neck and headaches and had been ripped out in chunks when I let my friends use it to climb down a steep mountain to escape from a goblin's lair. I was hoping that this time, there was a lot less hair.

My fingers found the back of my neck, which was completely free of hair. Yes! Whoever I was, it wasn't Rapunzel this time round. I poked around a bit more. OK, there was a short ponytail tied with what felt like a little velvet bow. I could live with that. I didn't even try to take off the bow although I would normally lie on the floor and have a Rory-style tantrum about it. The last time we were in Dralfynia, we had discovered that however hard we tried, we were stuck with the outfits that were worn by the characters we appeared to be.

Then I tried the top of my head. Hmm, there was a little crown there again, which meant I was someone royal. That was OK—I liked being royal—but this one wasn't as spiky as Rapunzel's crown had been. Nervously I opened my eyes and looked down. Awesome, I still had on my pink sneakers which I never, ever took off (OK, except when I went to bed, or went swimming, and stuff). Not so awesome: they now each had a big, shiny silver buckle on the toes. I checked myself out properly now and frowned.

"Why are you dressed as a boy?" Rory said to me. I didn't raise my eyes to look at him. I was too busy checking myself out because he was right. I was royal, so that was a good thing, but I was most definitely dressed as a boy.

Huh. Interesting.

"You think you've got a situation," Olive said. "Take a look at your brother over there."

CHAPTER 16

I followed the direction her finger was pointing. My eyes became round and so did my mouth. "No way," I whispered. Then I said, "So cuuuuuute." I dropped to a crouch and held my hand out toward Rory, gesturing with my fingers for him to come over to me. He ambled across, lay on his back with his legs in the air, and rolled from side to side as I tickled his furry little tummy. He gave little yelps of happiness, and when I tried to pull my hand away he grabbed at my arm with all four of his legs.

That's right. I counted them. He had four legs, no arms, and was covered in ginger fur. He was a bear. He was a baby bear. In fact, after I thought about it, I realized that he was *the* Baby Bear from Goldilocks and the Three Bears. He was seriously cute and cuddly. Well, until he opened his mouth that is.

"Ahem," coughed a voice from behind us. "Who are you and why is there a bear in the toilets of our inn?"

Ah. I understood. I had started my second strange saga in the bathrooms at school, and I was continuing it in the bathroom at the Inn of the Fluffy Kitten in Tylwyth Teg, a village in Dralfynia.

I looked at Aidan, the boy whose family owned the inn. He was standing in the doorway of the toilet looking at me dressed as a boy and playing with a little bear.

Not the best second impression I have ever made. Rory rolled over onto his feet (or do I mean paws?) and ambled across to my first crush.

"Hi Aidan," he said. Aidan went white. Even his freckles went white. His knees seemed to turn to straw and stopped supporting him. With his back to the doorframe, he slid down and landed firmly on his backside with his legs stretched out in front of him.

"A … a … a," he said. He raised a trembling finger and pointed at Rory. "A talking bear," he managed at last. The last time we were in Dralfynia we had seen a talking tree and a squadron of trained attack-bats as well as goblins and witches. A talking bear didn't seem like a very big deal compared to all that. "The sign was right," he added. He sounded amazed.

"What sign?" asked Rory. I was getting annoyed now. I had thought that Aidan would immediately recognize me and be pleased to see me. Instead he was talking to Rory about a sign.

"Hi Aidan," I interrupted. Then his eyes widened even more than they already had. I worried that they might pop out of his skull and go rolling across the straw-covered floor. He scrambled to his feet and spread his arms wide.

Oh boy! Not only did he recognize me straight away, he wanted to hug me! My first hug from a boy! I opened my arms too and stepped toward him. Then I quickly stepped back to avoid clashing heads with him as he suddenly bent down from the waist.

OK. I don't think I embarrassed myself too much, although I heard a little suppressed snigger from Olive behind me. I just had to hope that this was the Dralfynian version of a friendly hug. Aidan straightened up and looked at me expectantly. I wasn't sure what to do. Should I shake hands, hug him anyway, give a little wave?

Instead I bowed back.

"My prince," he said, shock in his voice. "You have no cause to bow to a commoner like me."

"Huh?" I said. "I'm not really a prince," I told him. "It's me, Sabrina. And that," I said pointing at Rory who was now throwing pawfuls of straw in the air and batting at them as they drifted back down. "That is Rory."

"And I am Olive," said Olive, walking across to stand next to me. She twirled a finger around one of the strange braids, trying to straighten it out. It didn't work; it bounced back like a spring and boinggged on the side of her head.

CHAPTER
17

Aidan had now had some time to work out what was going on. He ticked us all off on his fingers as he looked us up and down. "Where's the other one?" he asked suddenly. We all stood there and looked around. There was no sign of Persis. I glanced at Olive again.

"When you were dripping that stuff into our mouths, did you drip it in Persis' mouth?" I asked. Olive nodded. She had shoved us all into the cubicle, ignoring Rory's complaints about the girls' bathrooms being smellier than the boys' ones. Then she had said, "Don't ask any questions, just put this on your tongue, let it dissolve and think of safety." Then she'd grabbed our chins, tilted them up and started dripping from a little glass bottle. It had happened so fast that we didn't ask any questions but that would be happening soon, believe me.

"I did her first, then Rory, then me, and then you." She pointed at the pocket on my very smart, pink prince-jacket. I tugged down at it so that it looked better and absentmindedly I started to polish the pretty silver buttons with my sleeve. "I put the bottle in the pocket of your denim jacket when we were still back in Melas," she told me. I felt a lump and touched it. The half-empty bottle was still there. I pulled at my bottom lip while I thought about Persis.

"Maybe she got sent somewhere else. I mean, when you told us to think about safety, I thought of here because we came here after we escaped from Witchy Wu the first time, but perhaps she thought of her bedroom back home," I suggested. I looked at Aidan. I wondered if she had been scared to return after the goblins had kidnapped us last time. Perhaps her thoughts hadn't turned to Aidan straight away like mine had. "Yeah, I expect she went home instead of coming here," I concluded lamely.

"It is very strange that you came to this place, isn't it?" Aidan said. I wondered about the spells that had brought us here twice – there had been a watery link between back home Melas and over here in Dralfynia. Again, I wondered where Olive had gotten hold of a magic spell, but she interrupted me before I could ask.

"Well, Persis should have come to the same place as the rest of us," she said thoughtfully, "because we all started from the same place."

But she didn't get to say anything more because from a big heap of hay in a dark corner came the sound of rustling. I froze. It sounded like a whole family of rats to me. Then a massive, snorting snore filled the little hut, followed by a noise that sounded like someone using a chainsaw to cut down trees.

We hurried over and stared down. Persis lay on her back, one arm flung dramatically over her head and a peaceful smile on her face. She was deeply asleep. She looked so happy. I looked her up and down as she lay there. She wore a dress that was amazingly pretty. It was a delicate blue color and all shiny and shimmery and floaty. My silver buttons seemed plain in comparison. It seemed that Sleeping Beauty completed our funny little gang this time.

I gave a very deep sigh. "Here we all go again," I muttered. I gave Persis a gentle nudge with my foot, forgetting I had a silver buckle on my shoe. It scraped against her ankle and she woke up. I won't go into details of what she said but I can tell you that Persis/Sleeping Beauty is clearly not a morning person. We helped her get to her feet and pick straw from her hair. Now what?

"I think we need a meeting," I said. "Is it OK to come into the inn again?" I asked Aidan.

He bowed again and said, "For you, my prince, all things are possible." We all waited for a second for him to remember that I wasn't a prince. His face clouded, then cleared, and he said, "And anything is possible for you too, Sabrina." Then he blushed. I know because I looked carefully, and the gaps between his freckles were definitely a bit pink and his dimples were even deeper.

As we left the toilet, dragging a yawning Persis with us, I glared at Olive.

"I think we deserve an explanation," I said firmly. "I mean, thanks for saving us and all, but now it's time for you to come clean." She nodded meekly. I had my suspicions, of course, but I needed to hear from Olive where—or more specifically who— the magic potion had come from.

Aidan led the way as we crossed the yard that lead from the stable block and outdoor toilet to the Inn of the Fluffy Kitten. He glanced up at the wooden sign which had a rough painting of a very fluffy gray kitten on it. It was so fluffy that it looked like a pompom with toes and eyes. When I had last been there, I could have sworn that the kitten had moved when it thought I wasn't looking.

Rory was scampering around Aidan's feet as he walked, trying to pull with his teeth at the leather cords that were wrapped around Aidan's legs.

"Hey Aidan," he said. "Guess whose birthday it is today?" As he spoke the painted kitten sat bolt upright and let out a plaintive meow.

"A talking bear," squeaked the kitten. "I was right."

Ohhhh. I had thought he meant the kind of sign that a fortune teller had predicted. But, of course, this was Dralfynia: he had meant an actual living, moving, talking sign.

CHAPTER
18

Aidan sighed. "Yes, Twinkle, you were right," he admitted. He turned to us and explained. "Twinkle has dreams," he said. "Sometimes they are a bit, well, strange. You know what dreams are like, right?" We all nodded. Dreams usually make no sense. One minute you can be singing a hit song to the entire school wearing an astronaut outfit, the next you can be learning that your grandma's wig is really a chocolate cake.

Aidan was continuing. "Twinkle's dreams do occasionally come true," he said. He seemed a bit reluctant to talk about it.

"That's right," squeaked Twinkle. "Once I dreamed that Aidan's mom Jill would find her lost wedding ring in an apple pie she had baked. And I was right!" She jumped round in her sign excitedly, her little kitten tail held high and proud. "And then I dreamed that a talking bear would visit us, and I was right again."

"Wood visit us?" said Rory. Last time he had made a friend called Russell, a talking tree who loved terrible puns and lived in Scary Forest. Rory had been practicing his puns ever since. "Hey, let me axe you a question," he said. "Don't you get board?" He laughed, but Twinkle didn't understand puns so she took him at his word.

"Yes," she said sadly. "I'd like to get off the sign and go and visit the rest of my litter, but I got painted here and here I have to stay, all by myself. Still," she said, brightening up, "now I have you two to talk to as well." She started chasing her tail and doing little roly-polies.

Olive and Persis looked at each other, frowned, looked at the rest of us and then looked at each other again. "Uh," they chorused. "Why are you three talking to piece of wood?" Rory, Aidan and I stared back at them.

"Because it would be rude not to answer her," I said slowly. Wasn't it obvious? "Can't you guys hear her?" They shook their heads. "What about see her?" They nodded their heads.

"Sure, it's a painting of a kitten on a wooden sign," said Persis. "Hey, can we go inside? I'm so tired. I need to sit down."

"I meant, can't you see her moving around?" Persis and Olive shook their heads.

"Oh … they can't see me?" asked Twinkle. She thought for a second and then she stuck out her small pink tongue right at them, and giggled. Then she turned around so that her tail was pointing toward them and wiggled her furry little behind. Aidan shook his head, embarrassed.

"Sorry," he mouthed.

"Sorry for what?" Olive and Persis wanted to know.

"Never mind," I said. I looked up again at Twinkle, who was strutting back and forth in her sign, waving at Olive and Persis as she did so. "What else happened in your dream?" I asked her.

"Wouldn't you like to know?" she said, then giggled again.

"Twinkle," Aidan said in a firm voice, "please answer Sabrina's question. Oh, and by the way, they can't see you but we can."

"Who's 'Sabrina'?" Aidan pointed at me in reply. "Don't be silly; that person looks like Prince Charming," said Twinkle. "Anyone can see that." That sparked an idea. I straightened up and tried to look regal.

"You are correct," I said in my most fancy voice. "And, as Prince Charming, I order you to answer my question." Twinkle rolled onto her back so that all four of her legs were in the air.

"Sorry," she said. "I get excited when my dreams come true." She bounced to her feet again. "Let me see," she said, and sat down, curling her tail around her. "Dreams are hard to remember afterwards," she reminded us, "but there was a talking bear who visited me. Then he was gliding along as if he was sitting on something that floated." Rory and I looked at each other. That sounded just like Ruggy. Olive had picked up Ruggy from the outside toilet and was carrying him now. "And then it gets a bit muddled up, but there was a hand that only had one thumb and one finger on it trying to grab something that the bear wanted. Oh," she said, happily, "it was pretty and shiny. It sparkled." She gave a little mew of joy. "It was a glass slipper," she said. "It twinkled in the sunlight. I'd love to play with that," she added wistfully. "Or a butterfly; I'd love to play with a butterfly."

She had lost her train of thought.

"Then what happened in the dream?" I prompted her.

"What dream?" asked Olive and Persis, by now totally confused and a little bit irritated because we were ignoring them. Twinkle settled down into a comfortable position, wrapping her tail around her legs, and gave a yawn.

"I can't remember," she said. "There was that horrid witch, the one who eats children." She gave a little shiver. "That witch scares the splinters off me," she said "And the king and queen were there too," she continued, and gave another yawn. She closed her eyes and snuggled down. "Everyone was at the Island of Merthyr. It was very crowded in my dream. But the twinkly thing and the floaty thing were safe there, with the other thing." She opened one orange eye and looked at me with it. "That's the real king and queen, by the way. Not a pretend royal like you." She shut her eye and fake-snored. We couldn't get her to answer any more questions. She was bored with us now.

I felt a bit hurt that a kitten had seen through my Prince Charming impression so easily.

CHAPTER
19

We sat inside the Inn of the Fluffy Kitten. We were at the same table we had sat at before. A fire roared in the corner and there were plates of bread and cheese, cakes, and jugs of milk in front of us. It felt very cozy and familiar. It was cleaner and tidier than on our first visit, and Olive must have been pleased that the innkeepers had carried on with her good work. But however relaxed we felt, we all knew that we were right at the start of another strange saga and we had a lot to talk about.

"Why can't we see and hear the talking kitten sign?" asked Persis, pointing to herself and Olive. I shrugged. I didn't know and, to be very honest, I didn't want to think about it. A few things were starting to fall into place inside my head and I had a horrible feeling that I wouldn't like the answer they would add up to.

I told them what Twinkle had said and we tried to make sense of her dream.

"It's strange that the hand only had a thumb and one finger," I said.

Aidan nodded. "It can't mean the prince," he said. "Did you know that the Beast with Nine Fingers is now known as the Beast with Eight

Fingers?" he asked us. I blushed. Yes I knew. I had chopped another one of his fingers off when he tried to pull me from Ruggy last time we were in Dralfynia. "So," Aidan continued, "he still has a thumb and two fingers on his left hand."

"For now," said Olive. We all looked across at her. "I mean, if the kitten's dream was a kind of prophecy—you know, that the things she dreamed will come true—then at some time in the future, the Beast-prince guy must lose another finger." They all looked at me.

"Hey," I protested. "It was an accident, OK?" Surely I couldn't mistakenly cut off another finger—could I?

The inn was not busy, so Aidan had time to sit down with us. We filled him in on our adventures with Witchy Wu, and he told us what had been happening while we were back in Melas.

"In the three months you've been away," he began. Our eyes bugged out and our mouths dropped open.

"Three months?" we all said together. No wonder I had been shivering in the outdoor bathroom of the inn. I twisted and glanced out of the window. It was already starting to get dark and I could just make out that the leaves on the trees were gold and red. Fall was well underway, even though it had been late summer last time we came. We had been away for less than a week and a whole season had gone by in Dralfynia.

Aidan carried on as if we had not interrupted him. "In the three months you've been away, there've been a lot of changes in Tylwyth Teg. In fact, all across Dralfynia." He picked up a bread roll and began to tear little pieces off it, flicking them onto a wooden plate absentmindedly. "The Beast has been collecting his friends and putting together an army. The word is that he knows where your magic carpet is," he said nodding at Ruggy, who was now stretched out in front of the fireplace. "He's been saying that if he has any of the magic objects, he will arrange for Princess Heidi is declared dead and he will take over the kingdom, whatever the traditions say. He is certain he will be able to bully his parents into agreeing with him." His hands shook as he shredded his bread.

"Bad things have been happening," he said. His voice was a whisper. "People who have been loyal to the Duchess Yvonne and the old king and queen have disappeared." He looked around him nervously, as if the shadows hid spies. "Because you have one of the three magical objects that Prince Donaldo needs to become king, your lives are in terrible danger."

Our lives were in danger? That was starting to feel normal for us.

"Is there any honey?" said Rory. His tummy gave a growl.

"Or oatmeal?" added Olive.

"Is it bedtime yet?" finished Persis. I ignored them. I knew that they would all step up when I needed them. In the meantime, I still needed some answers from Olive before we decided what to do next.

"So, Olive," I began, staring at her. She immediately turned red and began to fiddle with her flicky braid.

"Mmmmm?" she said casually, looking up at the ceiling.

"So, Olive, how did we end up in Dralfynia? Again?" I demanded.

Persis chimed in. "Yeah, good question. I mean, I thought we'd seen the last of this place," she said, waving her hand around. "No offence, by the way," she added for Aidan's benefit, "but it isn't my idea of a fun way to spend a few days." She lifted up a fistful of the delicate material that her dress was made of, and then let it fall. "I mean, look at this outfit," she complained. Persis usually wore sweatpants or shorts, and t-shirts. Her thick black hair was usually pulled into a pony tail. Now it hung loose, swept over one shoulder. She joined me in staring at Olive. Rory lifted his hind leg and scratched at his side—then he looked at her too. Just how did we end up in Dralfynia this time?

CHAPTER
20

Olive blushed and stammered all the way through her story. She told us all about how she had met Bridget and told her that Witchy Wu had followed us; then she explained how Bridget had made a potion for us to take when we were all together, standing by some kind of water, in this case, a toilet.

"But at least we won't be here for long," she said, returning our stares. "The potion only lasts until dawn of our third day in Dralfynia and then, as long as we are standing by water, it doesn't matter where we are or what we are doing, we get sent back to the same place we were when we took the potion."

If she thought that would cheer us up, she was wrong. I didn't want to be in Dralfynia at all, never mind for that long. And then I started to think about everything else she had told me.

She had gone behind my back, told my stepmother what had happened and asked her for help. I couldn't believe it. Just as I was starting to trust Olive 'Ayres-and-Graces', she had betrayed me. It was just like the time when she told the teacher that it was me who had been talking in class when we should have been working, (I know, hard to believe I couldn't stop talking, right?) It was the truth, but she shouldn't have told.

Olive leaned forward, talking fast. I could tell she was trying to put things right, but I was too angry to listen.

"Brina, we needed help, you must understand that. We were in way over our heads. We all could have been killed. I tried to talk to you about it," she reminded me. "You know how annoying it is in movies when someone doesn't tell someone else a secret, or how they feel about them, but there's no logical reason for it? Except to make the movie longer?" Of course I'd seen movies like that so I understood what she meant, but I didn't nod. I was mad and getting madder the more she made excuses. She sat back on the wooden bench with an annoyed huff of breath. "So anyway, Bridget told me that as long as Ruggy was in Melas you and Rory were in danger."

I was feeling so angry that my jaws ached because I was clenching my teeth so hard. Then Olive said the worst thing of all.

"Sabrina Summers, what would you have done?" she asked suddenly. "What would you have done if you could see a new friend that you cared about was in danger, and was refusing to do anything to help herself out of it?" A little part of my brain told me that I would have done the exact same thing but luckily the stubborn, pig-headed part of my brain is much stronger and quickly closed down the thought. Instead, I looked for the only negative I could think of.

"Huh, well we're still in danger anyway, aren't we? So your dumb plan didn't exactly save us after all." My words were spiteful; they didn't make any sense, and worse, I had spoken them in front of Aidan. I rose to my feet and held out my left arm with the elbow crooked. "Come on," I told Persis. She stood up and placed her hand on my arm. "We'll be in the same room as before," I told Aidan. And, just like the prince and princess we appeared to be, we swept regally across to the wooden staircase.

Unfortunately, the staircase was too narrow to take us side by side. First, we got stuck. Then I tried to go first (I wasn't used to old-fashioned gallantry), but Persis tried to push through at the same time, so we got stuck again. I paused and said, "Ladies first then, I suppose." Persis gave a snort that sounded very much like a pig and not a lady; she shoved me out of the way, swept the long train of her dress up and over her shoulder, and stomped up the wooden stairs. I wasn't sure if she was irritated because she was tired, because she was in Dralfynia again, because she was a girly princess and I was the prince, or because I was squabbling with Olive again.

When we got to the room, it looked just the same as before. There were straw-filled mattresses and soft blankets made out of wool that was woven from the brushed fur of rescued stray cats. Persis flung herself dramatically down on one and turned her back to me.

"Is something up?" I asked. She didn't answer.

"What's the matter?" I tried again.

"Nothing."

"Are you OK?"

"I'm fine."

I gave up and decided to be thankful that I would never be a husband.

She fell asleep straight away, of course. I listened to the chainsaw noises coming from her. A little later I heard Olive quietly come into the room and settle down on one of the other mattresses. I felt bad that we had argued again, but for now I felt even worse about something else. It was something I could help with, though. When the Inn of the Fluffy Kitten was dark and everyone was asleep, I sneaked back down to the main room. Rory was curled up on Ruggy in front of the fire. The dull embers threw just enough light for me to see. I rummaged around behind the bar until I found what I was looking for. A paintbrush and a pot of bright blue paint.

I opened the front door and crept out. The moon was high in the sky, and offered a cold, silver glow. Twinkle was sleeping, but opened one eye to see what I was doing. I stood on tiptoes and dipped the brush into the paint pot. In a few minutes I had finished, and I turned to go back into the inn.

"Thank you," said Twinkle quietly. I smiled as I glanced back and saw one paw reach out for the ball of yarn that I had painted onto her sign.

CHAPTER
21

I didn't sleep very well. My brain was like a grasshopper, jumping from thoughts of Olive and Bridget, to Twinkle's dream, to where we should hide Ruggy, and finally to wondering what had upset Persis the night before.

I was the first to wake up. I was still tired, but I was restless at the same time. I got up quietly, pulled my pink prince-jacket straight, checked my crown was at a jaunty angle and headed outside. There was a light frost underfoot and my footsteps crackled as I stepped on the white grass. I could hear the early birds getting their worms, a deep neigh from a horse I couldn't see hidden somewhere deep in the Inn's cozy stable and the sound of a light breeze rustling though the leaves. It was lovely. I decided to go for a walk.

Tylwyth Teg looked peaceful in the morning light. The early morning sunshine made the frost sparkle like tiny diamonds and hardly anyone else was up and about yet. I could see my breath and I had fun puffing clouds of breath out into the cold air. I felt as though I had the whole place to myself and I took the chance to explore the village properly this time. Most of the little houses were neat and well kept. The thatch on the roofs was trimmed and the doorsteps were swept. Others looked empty and abandoned; I wondered if the families who lived there had just gotten up one night and left or if they had stood up to the Beast and been captured. The deserted homes were spooky.

I passed a bigger building and when I peeked in the window, I decided that it must be the school. There were lines of low benches and I could see squares of flat, thin dark stone, which had chalk writing and numbers on them. It looked dusty and neglected.

I kept strolling and found a group of larger buildings. When I peered in through the window of one of them, I decided it must be a kind of meeting hall as there were benches pulled into a ring with a throne pushed to one wall, ready to be pulled out when it was needed. The last of the bigger buildings that I checked out had mattresses laid out in rows. There were stacks of wooden boxes filled with rolls of bandages and glass bottles. It must be a hospital, I thought, but I couldn't imagine why it was so big for such a small village.

"We're getting ready," said Aidan from behind me. He made me jump. I turned around to look at him. He was carrying a wooden pole across his shoulders. It was carved to fit snuggly against his neck. From each end dangled a wooden pail filled with milk.

"That looks heavy," I said reaching to help him.

"No, it's OK; my, um, horse will help," he began, but I wanted to be useful, so I took one of the pails and immediately the other slid downward, spilling some of the milk.

"Oops sorry," I said. "I guess you were balanced." He nodded. "Wow, you really work long hours," I told him. When we had gone to our room last night, Aidan still had to clear the table before he could go to bed—and now here he was, getting milk first thing in the morning. Carefully he put the pails of milk down on the ground and wriggled his shoulders.

"It didn't used to be so hard for us peasants, Your Highness," he said. There was bitterness in his voice but then he laughed and I thought maybe he was teasing me. "But it's true. Ever since, well …" He paused as he carefully chose his words. "Ever since King Michael and Queen Hazel retired, the Beast has taken more and more power. Even though Duchess Yvonne is officially in charge, anyone who stands in his way is thrown into prison in Timaru Castle, including a good friend of mine. Last summer, the Beast got even worse. He suddenly raised taxes to pay for his own private army of goblins and soldiers. They come to villages like this and demand more and more money." He pointed to the milk. "We used to pay someone to help us at the inn but we can't afford to anymore. And hardly anyone comes to eat at the inn because they it costs them too much."

I didn't understand.

"Isn't he pretty rich already?" I asked. "I mean, what does he need more money for?" Aidan turned his eyes to the building behind me.

"He's raising an army," he told me. "That's why we needed to build a hospital. War is coming to Dralfynia."

CHAPTER
22

Well, being back in Dralfynia was not exactly fun this time round, either. So far I had:

1. traveled from toilet to toilet—yuk;
2. been betrayed by Olive;
3. squabbled with Olive;
4. started to worry that my little brother had fleas;
5. been ignored by Persis for no reason that I could understand;
6. shown myself up in front of Aidan; and
7. started to worry that Aidan blamed us for bringing civil war closer to Dralfynia because we took Ruggy away from the Beast. Sure, he was a prince, which might be enough for some people, but this guy really wanted to be king.

I wasn't at all happy as I trudged back to the Inn of the Fluffy Kitten, carrying one of the pails for Aidan and ignoring his insistence that he already had someone to help him. I had heard clopping hooves in the streets but there had been no sight of the horse he mentioned. Although

71

I had never chosen to visit Dralfynia, I was almost starting to like it and I felt guilty. I felt like I had to do something to make things right.

When we got back to the inn, I saw Twinkle playing with her ball of yarn. She lay on her back and used all four paws to spin the ball round and round and round. She looked very happy and I knew that I had made a positive difference for at least one Dralfynian.

Aidan nodded at the sign. "Thanks for doing that," he said. "That was really nice of you." I smiled at him but he looked serious. "I was really hoping that Twinkle's dreams weren't going to come true," he said. "They are the reason we think that a battle is coming soon," he explained. I hoped that Twinkle was wrong and her dream was nothing more than a chocolate cake wig instead.

I decided that I needed another list. Not one that told me what had gone wrong since I arrived in Dralfynia, but one where I could start to make things better—like with Twinkle's ball of yarn. I decided to start small with my list of "putting things right." Rory was sitting on Ruggy and scratching his belly. Orange hair drifted like a cloud around him. I got some soap from Aidan and took Rory out to the yard. There was a water trough and a pump. I had to push the handle up and down a few times but then the water came out and Rory splashed it all over himself. I rubbed soap into his fur while he giggled and wriggled, and splashed me; we had a great time. I rinsed him off, pleased with my work.

"Take that, fleas," I said. Then I watched in horror as Rory ambled over to a big pile of what I hoped was mud—and rolled around and around on it.

I came close to giving up on my list then but I decided to count it as a success and hoped that any fleas still left after the scrubbing had been squashed by Rory rolling around.

I carried on and next up were Olive and Persis. I went back upstairs and found Persis sitting on an upturned bucket as Olive fussed with her hair, trying to give her ringlets. I shook my head in disbelief. Persis with ringlets? Even when she was little and her mother had tried to make her have her hair curled, she had refused.

I coughed from the doorway so that they would notice me. They looked up and saw me. They both froze.

"We need to talk," I said. They both started talking at once. I raised my voice.

"I mean, I need to talk," I said. They both stopped talking and just looked at me, waiting. Why was this so hard? They were my friends; it should be easy. I forced myself on.

"So I have a couple of things to say—and then Olive, you can speak and then Persis, you can speak. We take it in turns and listen to each other, OK?" They nodded.

"OK, here goes. Olive, I know you meant well and if I had been in your shoes, I might have done the same thing. You were looking out for all of us." Olive opened her mouth to interrupt me, but I raised a finger. It was still my turn. "But," I continued, "I felt hurt that you didn't tell me what was going on. Although I know I made it difficult, I wish you hadn't tricked me into coming to Dralfynia." Before she could answer, I switched my attention to Persis and hurried on with my speeches. If I stopped now, my nerve might fail me so I had to keep going. "Persis, I have no idea what I did that made you suddenly go all moody last night. If you have something to say, please just tell me instead of playing silly games."

Persis' mouth dropped open, then snapped shut.

"You ate the last piece of cake last night," she muttered. "And you paid way more attention to Aidan than to me," she added.

"Women," I thought to myself. "I'll never understand them."

"Sabrina," said Olive, "I'm sorry. I know I let you down, but there was a witch in our school and I was scared. Next time …" Persis and I both gulped and shook our heads before she could continue.

"No 'next times' for finding witches at school, please," I said in a faint voice. At least it brought a tiny smile to Olive's face.

"Anyway, we have bigger problems, I'm afraid," I told them. "Aidan says that war is coming and I think it's because we stole Ruggy. We need to either hide him like Twinkle said, on the Island of Merthyr with the old king and queen; or," I took a deep breath. This was going to be hard to say, and I couldn't even believe that I had thought it.

"Or, we need to give Ruggy to the Beast and prevent a war."

CHAPTER
23

I inched back slightly, expecting Persis and Olive to start yelling their objections. Instead, they exchanged a look. Now it was my mouth that dropped open and snapped shut. Like Persis had, I looked like a fish at feeding time.

"Had you already thought of that?" I accused them.

"Well, yes we had actually," said Olive. She folded her arms across her chest and jutted her jaw. "It's the logical thing to do. The fact that we have Ruggy makes it really dangerous for us and our families, and for the people at school. That poor Princess Heidi must be dead or she would have come back, there's no-one to stand up to him. Eventually he's going to win. Why not save ourselves a world of trouble and get it over with—and then go home?"

I had been wondering the same thing. Why not? Why did I want to stay and at least make sure Ruggy was safe? I didn't have an answer but someone else did. I heard a scrape of claws on the wooden floorboards behind me. In spite of his little legs and round tummy, Rory had managed to climb the stairs and now stood behind me.

"Why? Because we can make a difference," he said. He was using his best, growly bear voice. "Dad always told us that bad things happen because good people like us don't stop it. I think we have to find the shiny thing that was in Twinkle's dream, and take it and Ruggy to the king and queen where they will be safe." I looked at him amazed.

"You listened to what Dad said?" I asked.

"He does say the same things over and over," he pointed out. "Some of it was bound to stick." Talking of sticking, Rory's fur was full of twigs, dried leaves and little seed pods. I think he was enjoying being Baby Bear.

Persis interrupted.

"As a matter of fact," she said, "that's what Olive and I had decided as well. I mean, the logical thing is to give Ruggy to the Beast and go home and pretend none of this happened." She gave an unhappy sigh. "But the way those goblins and Witchy Wu treated us makes me really angry," she said.

"And I hate the way that everyone is so scared all the time," added Olive. "That must be a terrible way to live: never knowing if you're going to have enough to eat, or if you'll be put in prison for disagreeing with someone."

I guess we had all decided that we were going to do "something". Now all that we had to do was to decide what it was, and then actually do it.

Easy!

But it turned out that it wasn't going to be easy, not at all.

We started with "deciding what to do" and we went to see Twinkle, collecting Aidan on the way. The sun was high and it was much warmer now. It was a good day to be starting on an adventure. Twinkle listened to us explain that we thought we needed to take Ruggy and the shiny thing to the Island of Merthyr. We wanted to know if we had understood her dream properly.

"Yeeees," she said slowly. She flicked a paw at a leaf that drifted past her sign. "Do you know what the shiny thing is? I couldn't really see it in my dream." We nodded. The second magical object that the rightful rulers of Dralfynia needed was a glass slipper. I told her that. Twinkle scratched behind her ear with one of her back legs.

"There are two glass slippers, of course," she said. "I mean, it would be pointless to have just one glass slipper, wouldn't it? Who would want just one shoe? It's the Beast with Eight Fingers, not the Beast with One Foot," she pointed out, chuckling at her own joke. She had a point. I had never thought about it that way before. "There's one slipper nearby, you know. The Old Woman Who Lives in a Shoe has it in her collection," Twinkle told us. Then her head began to nod, her eyes began to close and she was almost instantly fast asleep.

"What's she saying now?" asked Persis.

"Nothing, she's gone to sleep." I reached up my hand and gently rocked the swinging sign. It moved gently, like a baby's cradle. Twinkle didn't wake up.

"Hey Twinkle, there's another cat over there," Aidan said in a loud voice. Twinkle was up on her paws, fur standing on end and tiny sharp teeth exposed in a snarl before he finished his sentence.

"Hsssss, this is my territory—mine," she said. She looked around and saw that there was no other cat.

"Hah, I scared it off," she said, and gave her paws a victory lick.

"The other glass slipper?" I prompted her.

"Mmm? Oh, the other one is lost. You need them both of course. And yes, the magical objects will be safe with the king and queen, but I don't know why, nor for how long." She spat out a shred of blue yarn that had been stuck between her teeth. I translated what she said to Olive and Persis. How would we ever find a single glass slipper hidden somewhere in the whole of Dralfynia in the short amount of time we had left before Bridget's potion returned us to Melas?

"As a matter of fact," said Olive. "I know exactly where the other glass slipper is." We all stared at her stunned. How could she possibly know that?

CHAPTER
24

"**B**ecause I tidied it away when I was Cinderella the last time we were here," she explained. She had done a lot of cleaning and tidying up when we were last in Dralfynia, just as she kept wanting porridge, or oatmeal, now that she was Goldilocks, and Persis kept yawning now that she was Sleeping Beauty.

"I put it on a shelf in the goblins' cave where we were held captive," she explained.

Of course! Where else would it be, except for the most dangerous place in the entire land of Dralfynia? I gave a little sigh as I tried to work out a plan.

"We need to go get the first glass slipper from the Old Woman Who Lives in a Shoe, then we need to go back to the goblins' lair and get the other one. And then we need to come back here and go to the Island of Merthyr with the slippers and Ruggy. And all by ..." I twisted my mouth as I did the math.

There was a long pause, and I was still counting on my fingers behind my back when Olive said, "Dawn, on the day after tomorrow."

Twinkle interrupted. "The Old Woman Who Lives in a Shoe is

called Latrina Earwax," she told us. "She'll never sell you that shoe. She has it hidden away. One of my friends is her 'Open/Closed' sign, and she told me."

Aidan had been quiet so far, but now he spoke.

"The only way to make it work is to split up," he said. "One group will have to go to the goblin's cave and the other one will have to visit the shoe museum here to get the slipper from old Latrina Earwax. Then you'll all have to meet back here and hire a boat to row over to the Island of Merthyr. There's no other way to get it done in the time you have. And, although I'd like to help," he continued, suddenly speaking very quickly, "I'm going to have my own adventure." I looked around at the Inn of the Fluffy Kitten. It didn't seem very adventurous to me. But that wasn't what he meant. "One of my friends, Ellie, has been captured by the Beast. She was part of a group of us who used to meet to find ways to stand up to the Beast and the goblins. Someone betrayed her, and I'm going to go and rescue her."

He kept looking at us as he spoke, as if we should be offering to help.

There was a long silence until I spoke. "If we had more time …" I began.

"I guessed you'd say that," he said bitterly. "Even though it's because of your visit here that she's in the tower," he added. We were stunned. We had no idea what he was talking about, nor why he was so angry. "All the help you had from me, from Russell and from Clyde—doesn't that mean anything to you?" He was becoming even angrier now and we didn't understand what we had done. "We all put our lives in danger for you. You just turned up, dressed as some of our own people and then left again without caring about the mess you left behind." I was so shocked that tears needled at the back of my eyeballs. I hated to think that we had done anything as terrible as Aidan seemed to think we had.

"Please," I said, "please just tell us what's happened and what we can do to make it right."

So he did.

He explained to us that anyone who helped those people who stood up to the Beast was likely to be put in the prison within Timaru Castle. We knew it well. We had been to Dralfynia's capital city already and had been captured ourselves. He told us that Ellie had been seen rescuing us from a dungeon in that castle—and a few days later, the Beast's goblin army had come to arrest her. I interrupted him.

"This Ellie girl didn't rescue us," I said, surprised. "It was Olive." He nodded excitedly. At last we were about to understand his point.

"It was Olive, that's true. But she was dressed as Cinderella. Whoever betrayed her thought that she was the real Cinderella, the girl we call Ellie."

Oh.

Ah.

Not good.

"So, it's our fault that your friend is in the tower, isn't it?" Aidan shrugged in a way that meant, "Yes, but I am too polite to say so, and you have to figure it out for yourselves anyway."

OK. So now we had to search a shoe museum shaped like a giant shoe, burglarize a goblins' cave, rescue the real Cinderella, and then get ourselves and the magic objects back to Tylwyth Teg so we could row across to the Island of Merthyr before dawn on the third day after we arrived.

No problem.

CHAPTER 25

"Right," I said, looking at the rest of them. They looked back at me. "Right," I said again. I sucked in a breath between my teeth and stared up at the sky, trying to think of how to begin.

"Maybe if we started by splitting the teams?" prompted Olive.

"I was just going to say that," I interrupted, irritated.

"I have a suggestion," Aidan offered. He pointed at Rory who was wandering around snuffling under the fall leaves that lay in piles in the yard. "The goblins like watching dancing bears, so I think Rory would easily be able to get into their lair." Bears that danced? It sounded very strange. He saw the confusion on my face. "They are very cruel," he reminded us. "They like to watch animals being poked and hurt for fun." Rory had wandered over to join us. It was hard to tell what he was thinking because, well, he was a bear, but he made me proud when he spoke up. It's not a feeling I am used to, by the way.

"Well perhaps this bear will cause a bit of trouble while he's in there, then." His voice was suddenly growly and his eyes, which were brown like hot chocolate, looked fierce. Then Olive spoke up.

"I think I should go with Rory," she said. "It makes sense because I'm Goldilocks, and so it fits with the story. And a prince rescued Sleeping Beauty in the old stories, so you and Persis go together anyway. Plus the glass slipper was found by Prince Charming so you two should go get the other glass slipper. Then we'll all meet in Timaru."

I could tell she didn't want to go with me but I didn't want to go with her either, and I thought that Persis needed me to look after her. I was silent while I pretended to think it through, and then I said, "Sure; why not?" None of us came up with a "why not", even though we tried. "Sooooo, we just split up now and go our own ways then?" I asked. And after an hour or so of fussing and getting food from Aidan's mom's kitchen, that's just what we did.

I caught Olive by the arm as she and Rory were getting ready to leave.

"Hey, you know Rory's dyslexic?" She nodded. "It helps him if you break a plan into little pieces and get him to do one part of it at a time. He gets kind of stressed if you try to get him to remember heaps of stuff all at once."

"OK," she said. It would be no big deal, really. All she would have to do was think about it, be patient and make sure Rory felt in control. Then she said, "You're a good big sister." Huh, she was right for once. And not to get too sentimental, I almost felt frightened and upset because Rory wasn't going to have me to look out for him—but don't tell him that. And I definitely did not have a tear in my eye as I watched them walking out of the yard and away. Their journey would begin with finding a quiet spot with no one around and then jumping onto Ruggy who would fly them right to the goblin's lair.

Our plan was way less dangerous, I thought. I decided that rather than try to steal this particular glass slipper, I would just saunter up to the Old Woman Who Lives in a Shoe, act like a prince and demand my property back. Then we'd borrow a cart and arrive in Timaru in some style. I told Persis and Aidan what I was going to do, and said to Persis,

"You stay here and rest, my dear. I'll collect you afterwards. It may be dangerous. I need to look after you." She gave me a look that said "Look after yourself, loser," and strode out of the yard toward the center of the village. This prince and princess thing was really kind of silly.

"Is she going the right way?" I asked Aidan, while we watched her grow smaller as she disappeared into the distance. He shook his head.

"No, she's going totally the wrong way," he said.

CHAPTER 26

After we had called Persis back, the three of us skirted the edge of Tylwyth Teg and headed in a direction we hadn't been before. It was a beautiful day and the walking was easy. We passed fields of enormous pumpkins, already harvested and waiting to be taken to market. They were much bigger than the ones we had seen the last time we were in Tylwyth Teg. One was so huge that it hid an entire animal; all we could see was a pair of furry, brown ears peeping over the top of it. There were little white houses dotted along the route. One had a garden filled with flowers that buzzed and shook with clouds of bees. Big pottery jars of honey were stacked outside.

"How much are they?" I asked Aidan.

"How much what?" he said.

"Money. How much money do they cost?" I thought Rory would like one.

"Munny?" He said the word as if he had never heard it before. "Only rich people have money these days," he told us. "We have been so heavily taxed we have nothing left. We just trade or share what we need. We try to make sure none of us goes without." I couldn't even imagine a world like that, it seemed so strange. I wondered how much more damage the Beast would do if he came to power and when a cloud went in front of the sun, I shivered.

Soon we came to a wide grassy field. A path of gray cobblestones led from the road we were walking along to a great big boot. It was the size of some of the small homes we had passed. There was a door painted a cheerful red in the middle of it, where your ankle would go if you had great big feet. A little window was placed where your toes would start and another window was higher up where your socks would fold over. I knew we had come to see someone called the Old Woman Who Lived in a Shoe, but I hadn't actually expected an item of footwear to be her home. There was a little sign shaped like a small boot with the words:

Shoe Museum
Home for unfashionable shoes,
single shoes missing their partner,
shoes that give blisters, clogs and other ugly,
unwanted and unloved shoes, sandals and boots.
We never turn away a shoe in need of a home—
not even smelly ones.
Donations welcome.
We are: OPEN

I realized that the sign was Twinkle's friend when two of the shoes painted onto it suddenly gave a little tap dance.

"We're here," said Aidan. I nodded. I had figured that much out. "I'll stay here," he said. "I know Latrina from when she visits the village; it'll seem strange if I come with you."

"I'll stay too," said Persis. "I could do with a nap after that long walk."

She sat down on some grass and I started up the path and went to knock on the door. It had a brass door knocker on it. Guess what it was shaped like? That's right, a shoe. It had a dainty little heel and a bow on the toe. I tried to lift it up and bang it down, but it was fixed firmly in place. I gave up and rapped on the door with my knuckles instead. While I waited, I tried to imagine what a woman who collected unloved shoes would be like. I pictured a pink-faced old lady with a mass of white hair, a frilly, flowery apron and a nice smile. She would probably smell of home baking. But I was getting used to being wrong about almost everything in Dralfynia, and this time was no different.

The person who opened the door was very tall with a face as brown and shiny as polished leather. She wore a long dress that shimmered gold and green, and her hair was wiry, like a big tangled mess of shoelaces.

She loomed over me with a frown. My confidence took one look at her and ran away to hide. "Um," I said. She tilted her head down in a greeting that was sort of a bow, although her strange, green eyes never left my face.

"Welcome, Your Highness, to my little museum," she said. She pulled the door open and gestured grandly with her free arm. I stepped inside.

Oh boy, the smell! It was the worst smell of sweaty feet I have ever smelt. It crept up my nose and when I tried to breathe through my mouth, I could actually taste it. I was glad that Olive with her infamous weak stomach wasn't around for this. Actually, I wished she was and I wasn't, but I was trying to be nice.

"I believe you are Mrs. Earwax? It's quite warm in here, isn't it?" I said, looking at the windows hopefully. "Perhaps some fresh air?"

"Oh no, Your Highness," she said. "This shoe museum is climate controlled to protect the exhibits." I was surprised that the exhibits hadn't just run away by themselves.

CHAPTER
27

She wanted to show me around, so I let her. I had expected her to just show me the glass slipper because I was Prince Charming, and I would then demand she hand it over straight away.

I had never been to a shoe museum before and I hope I never go to one again. The little room had a wooden spiral staircase which I guessed led up to her bedroom, but every other space was filled with shelves of shoes. Each shoe was boring. They were all tatty and worn out, and either brown or black in color. They were terrible shoes. Anyone else in our world, as well as in Dralfynia, would have thrown them out. Yet Latrina Earwax told me the story of every shoe in that place in terrible, mind-numbing detail. I learned who had made each shoe and whether the elves had helped the cobbler or if he had done it all by himself. She told me who had worn it and where Latrina had found it. If it was a pair of shoes, she told me the story twice, once for each shoe. I wanted to fall to my knees, fling my arms around her legs and beg her to stop.

But I didn't and so she didn't. She kept on going.

And going.

And going. I was getting desperate. There was no sign of any glass slipper anywhere. Then, my life was saved. There was a knock on the door. I rudely hurried across to open it and saw Persis standing outside, looking cross at having been kept waiting for so long. Then, the smell rolled out and hit her and she took several steps backward, fast.

"I was just wondering where you were," she said. Her voice squeaked because she was pinching her nose with her finger and thumb.

"I've been having a very interesting time," I said with no truth at all to my words. "Come in," I told her.

"No, no, no," she squeaked back. "Just, you know, hurry up and find the glass slipper—and let's get on our way."

Latrina Earwax was standing behind me listening. "Glass slipper?" she asked. "Oh Your Highness, have you been losing those glass slippers of yours again?" She waved her index finger at me as if I was a naughty toddler. Then she looked past me to Persis. "Isn't that the wrong princess?" she asked suspiciously. She was correct. Persis was Sleeping Beauty and the slippers are in the story of Cinderella.

I improvised. "Oh you know," I said casually. "Any old princess will do me. So, my glass slipper then?" I held out my hand. "I heard you had it in your collection, and you know what princesses are like. This one is dying to try it on and marry me," I said. I didn't dare look at Persis as I spoke. Latrina shook her head.

"No glass slippers here, I'm afraid." I had told a few fibs in my time. I wasn't proud of them, but it had taught me one thing: how to recognize when someone was telling me a fib. Latrina Earwax was lying to me. As I looked at her, I knew without doubt that somewhere in this strange building was the glass slipper. But how would we find it? She was a big, strong woman and she could easily stop us if she needed to. I knew that she had it hidden and we had to find it. The only way would be to get her out of the place first.

My hero Persis stepped up.

"Mrs. Shoe?" she began. I think she must have been snoozing when we had been told that the woman's name was Latrina Earwax. I saw the woman's green eyes flash with anger before her fake niceness was back in place.

"It's Mrs. Earwax, actually my dear. How can I help you?" I saw Persis' eyes tear up. I wasn't sure if it was the smell or if it was because she was trying not to laugh at the name.

"It's my servant," Persis continued. "He's very unwell. He's a boy we hired from the village. He has fainted by your front gate and I think you should uh, check him out or something. Please." I shook my head. Persis was not great at princess-speak. She would never fall for it.

She fell for it.

"How terrible. Really, servants these days just collapse at the first sign of hard labor for little or no reward. Please show me the way and I'll take care of him for you." She swept out of the room and shut the door behind her with me inside. I didn't have long. Gagging gently as I went, I hurried up the stairs and found a neat bedroom. I felt all through the bedding, searched all the drawers and cupboards and even peered into mouse holes and behind the curtains.

There was nothing. I peeked out of the window and saw Latrina Earwax and Persis bending over Aidan. For some reason he was soaking wet and there was an empty bucket next to him. There was a lot of talking and arm waving going on.

I ran back down to the museum and rummaged through all the exhibits, picking up each one and shaking it.

Nothing. The shoe museum was full of shoes, but not the one we needed.

CHAPTER 28

O live unfurled Ruggy and laid him on a patch of grass. They had walked for an hour or so until they were well clear of the village and the outlying farms. It had taken them twice as long as it should have. Rory kept gamboling off to chase after skittering fall leaves, rolling in heaps of freshly cut grass, and stopping to scratch his claws on tree trunks.

"I hope Ruggy still knows who you are," said Olive. She was worried. This plan was hopeless. There was no plan at all, really. They were making it up as they went along and the only person she had to help her was an extremely adorable, but easily distracted bear cub. Rory gave a little growl and Ruggy replied by giving a wriggle as if he was doing a Mexican wave. Carefully Olive stepped onto Ruggy and was immediately flipped off, landing on her back.

"Hey quit that," she said, annoyed. She scrambled to her feet. "We're in trouble again, Ruggy, and we need your help. I know you're happy to be home again, and we promise to get you to safety, but right now please just be good, OK?"

"He can't actually talk out loud, you know," said Rory. Olive closed her eyes and shook her head. She was talking to a carpet and taking advice from a bear cub. Her life had taken a very strange turn.

"Let's just get going," she said grumpily. She stepped carefully onto Ruggy again. Nothing happened. So far so good. She sat down and crossed her legs. Ruggy gave a big lurch and bucked her off so that she rolled over and over. Rory doubled up with laughter.

"I'd better get on first," he said, swiping tears from his eyes. "Ruggy trusts me." He walked onto the rug and gestured with his front paw for Olive to join him. She crawled on this time and gripped the fringe tightly. Ruggy didn't move.

"Tell him to fly to the goblin's mountain lair," she said to Rory. Rory repeated her words.

Ruggy didn't move.

"Seriously, this is the most uncooperative flying carpet ever," said Olive. Ruggy immediately lurched upwards at a terrific speed, leaving Olive's scream and Rory's roar of panic far behind in his slipstream. Rory's claws hooked into the fabric of the rug as he struggled to hold on with his paws, and Olive's legs flew out behind them as Ruggy continued on his vertical journey.

"Aaaaaaaahhhhhhh," said Olive. She closed her eyes tightly, too afraid to look down. "I'll barf on you if you don't start flying properly," she yelled. Ruggy's front end dipped down until he was flying horizontally again and Olive stopped feeling sick and hot and scared. After a few minutes' deep breathing and smooth, bump-free flying she started to enjoy herself.

"This is kind of fun, isn't it?" she said, looking at the countryside spread out like a map below them. "Dralfynia is a pretty land," she said.

"It's a kingdom," Rory corrected her. "It's ruled by a royal family, so it's a kingdom." He paused and then added, "I'd love to be a king. No one would be forced to go to school if it was a sunny day—and if they had problems, they'd get the lessons that helped them, not the same lessons everyone else had."

Olive thought about what he said and everything she had seen and heard so far in Dralfynia. It was interesting, very interesting.

"You'd be a great king," she said kindly.

"Totally," he agreed. "And Nathan and Heath would lead my army and navy, and we'd battle any other kingdoms that came near us." She didn't answer. She couldn't help but wonder if Rory's imaginings were a little close to the truth.

Their other journeys on Ruggy had been like trying to tame a wild mustang, but Olive's pep talk seemed to have done the trick for now. He was docile and calm, giving them a smooth ride as they skimmed over treetops and swooped low along the edge of Lake Pleasant. Behind them was the village of Tylwyth Teg. A dark shape in the middle of the lake was the Island of Merthyr, where the retired king and queen and some servants lived with their colony of rescued stray cats and kittens. An even darker smudge to the side was the beginning of Scary Forest, in the deepest, darkest part of which stood Witchy Wu's gingerbread cottage. When they last saw it, it had been a half-eaten pile of delicious crumbs. Purple mountains rose up ahead of them. This time they had snowy peaks, and Olive wondered if Dralfynians skied; she loved skiing. Beyond them lay Timaru.

The mountains were the home of the goblins who had kidnapped them last time they were in Dralfynia. It felt as though whichever direction she looked in, there was peril.

CHAPTER
29

I went out and rescued Aidan and Persis from Latrina Earwax, said, "Thank you for saving my servant" a whole heap of times, then we walked off along the road until we were out of sight and could stop and talk.

"Did you get it?" asked Persis excitedly. Aidan dragged his hands across his face and flicked away water. I shook my head.

"Nope. I don't know where it's hidden, but it's not inside that shoe-house place," I told them. I could tell by the way they were looking at me that:

(a) they were not impressed, and

(b) they both thought they could have found it if they had gone in there instead of me.

"So now what?" said Persis, sitting down on a rock.

"Tell me everything that went on in there," said Aidan as he twisted the ends of his shirt to wring it out. I was realizing that he was a person who needed all the details and to think things through instead of rushing in with no information like ... well, like me.

I told him about the door knocker being broken, about the smell and the boring exhibits, and about all the places I had searched.

"It's not very welcoming to have a museum that's full of terrible shoes and really smells bad," Persis remarked. "Especially if she can't even hear you knock."

"I guess she doesn't want any visitors," I agreed. Aidan nodded thoughtfully.

"She hardly ever comes into the village," he said. "Unless we need help looking for the sheep-stealers."

"Sheep-stealers?" asked Persis. Aidan nodded.

"We have a paddock where the village sheep live. We look after them, and in return they let us use their fleece for wool. Lately, every month something takes one of the sheep from under our noses. We don't know if it's a dragon, a wolf, goblins, or even people—but Latrina is always there to stand guard at night or go looking for the culprits the next day." He kicked at the small pebbles in the road, sending up clouds of dust. "It's a real problem for us," he admitted. "It's been happening for almost a year and we never catch them. It's as if they know when we're on guard or where we're hunting for them."

As I listened to him, two words jumped out at me. They were "dragon" and "wolf". Bats, goblins and attack-trees weren't enough? I wondered how many other creatures there were in Dralfynia who would be happy to take a bite out of us.

"Anyway," Persis interrupted, "when are we going to go back and get the slipper?"

"Well, if she almost never leaves her house, how can we go and look for it again?" I asked.

"We don't need her to leave," Aidan said, smiling at Persis and me. "It was right there in front of your nose all along."

We didn't speak for a few minutes as we tried to work it out, then Persis said, "Ooooohhhhhhh." Then they both looked at me, waiting patiently.

"Oh, just tell me," I said. Guessing games are for kids and I was way too mature to play; that was my excuse anyway.

CHAPTER
30

The higher Ruggy rose up the side of the mountain, the colder it got. Olive moved closer to Rory, being careful not to make Ruggy wobble too much. It was bliss. Rory was warm and furry, and great to cuddle up to. She leaned her head on his shoulder and sighed happily.

"What are you doing? I hate it when girls touch me. I might catch something," said Rory.

"I don't care," Olive said, snuggling deeper. "You're so comfy and cozy."

"Go away!"

"No."

"Yes.

"Make me." Olive was an only child who had no idea what she had let herself in for. Five seconds later she was trapped underneath Rory with her arms and legs flailing in the air being tickled and threatened with suffocation. As they fought, they hadn't noticed that Ruggy was bringing them nearer and nearer to their destination.

There was a little bump and suddenly they were down. He had landed them in a clearing that was very familiar. When they had escaped from the goblins and Witchy Wu by climbing down Sabrina's hair, they had run to this very clearing and Rory had discovered that Ruggy was a magical flying carpet.

They stood up, brushed themselves down, scowled at each other and then looked around. It was very quiet. There was no wind, no sound of birds cheeping or of small animals rustling, which Olive, for one, was grateful for.

"Now what?" said Rory. Olive remembered Sabrina's advice—they would take this one step at a time.

"First, I think we need to hide Ruggy here," she said. "That way, when we escape, we know right where to come and get him." Rory nodded, rolled Ruggy up nice and tight, hugged him goodbye, and leaned him up against a tree trunk. Then he hid him with some branches that had fallen from the trees. It would be almost impossible for anyone passing to see Ruggy at all, unless they tripped right over him.

"OK, now we go climb the rest of the mountain and say 'hi'," said Olive. "Can you actually dance?" she asked.

"Can I dance?" he scoffed. "Check out my moves!" He stood on his hind legs and shimmied his rear end. He raised one paw and extended one claw, pointing it up to the sky, while the other front paw pointed down. Then he started to jump up and down on the spot. His little tummy bounced in rhythm. Olive was doubtful.

"Well, it'll have to do. Just remember, no talking. If they find out you're a talking bear, they'll be so excited that they'll never let us go."

"So we just walk in, I do a dance while you get the slipper, and then we walk out?" Rory asked.

"Yes; we should be in and out in an hour at the most," said Olive with a confidence she did not feel.

"Why do they want to see me dance?" Olive shook her head.

"Believe me, I have no idea," she said honestly. "I'd rather not have seen it."

"I mean," said Rory heavily, "why do they want to watch bears dance?" She shook her head again.

"I don't know. Goblins are like some people; they like to laugh at animals or people by humiliating them, or hurting them."

"Like bullies?"

"Like bullies." This was turning out to be a complicated conversation. Olive wondered how other people coped with brothers and sisters. She'd always wanted a little sister who she could play with and dress up but she hadn't realized how tiring it was. Rory returned to his questioning.

"Maybe they'll pay us because I'm such a great dancer," he said.

"Maybe."

"I bet they will."

"I bet they will, too."

"Do you remember all that gold and stuff we stole and threw at them when we were escaping last time?"

"Uh-huh, I remember."

"I wonder if some of it's still here."

"I don't know."

"Do you think it is?"

"No."

"Why not?"

"Because they probably came and collected it all."

"What if they missed something?"

"If they missed something, we can pick it up on the way back to Ruggy."

As they had been talking, they had left the cover of the woods and started to climb up a steep, narrow, rocky path. Rory pattered along easily, sometimes ahead of her, sometimes behind her. Olive walked carefully, picking her way between stones. The drop to the side was steep and the valley below was full of jagged rocks.

"Are you scared of falling over?"

"Yes."

"Just run along like me."

"No thanks."

"Go on, it's easy. Look at me. Watch me."

"I said no."

"Go on … oops … ouch."

"Are you OK?"

"I did that on purpose."

"Oh."

"Are we nearly there?"

"Oh, thank goodness—yes we are."

CHAPTER
31

"So she does have the slipper after all," I said. "I wonder why she didn't tell me about it when I asked?"

"I guess she wants to keep it for herself," suggested Persis. "Whatever, we need to get it from her and it seems like we probably need to take it without asking," she added. "We don't have a lot of time and it doesn't really belong to her, anyway." That sounded a bit weak to me, but I knew she was right. We didn't have much time. We didn't even have time to wait until dark, which would have given us some protection. We just had to grab the slipper and get on our way as fast as we could.

We started off crawling on our hands and knees to keep below the height of the hedge that surrounded the field where Latrina lived. Unfortunately, Persis and I made too much noise complaining about the sharp stones that cut our palms and knees as we went, so we tried bending down low and hurrying along. Unfortunately, Persis and I made too much noise complaining about how it hurt our thighs.

Aidan got fed up with us.

"Why don't you just stand up and run as fast as you can?" he said. He pointed at my feet. "Your strange shoes look perfect for running in."

My pink sneakers were perfect for running in, even with the big, shiny buckles on them. If you ask me, these were the kind of shoes that should be in a shoe museum.

"OK, you know what to do?" I nodded. I knew what to do. I thought about running for first base when I was playing softball, chasing Persis and Rory when we played tag, and all the cross-country runs I had done at school. I'm competitive when it comes to sport—and almost as good as Persis if I'm on my best form. I could definitely do this. I stood up and looked at where I wanted to go. I lowered my head and I started to run.

I skidded around the corner from the road and onto the cobbled path heading right for the boot-shaped building. I pulled up, hardly even out of breath and I gripped the door knocker. Instead of trying to knock on the door with it though, I yanked at it with all my strength to pry it from the door. It hardly moved. I squinted at it and saw that it had been stuck in place with some kind of glue that had bits of hair in it. I looked around and saw a flat, pointed stone that was part of the path. I grabbed it and shoved it into the tiny gap between the heel and the door. I wiggled and pushed the stone with one hand, and pulled at the door knocker with my other hand. It was just starting to move but it was hard work and I was beginning to pant.

I heard footsteps on the other side of the door. I stopped straight away, hardly daring to breathe in case she heard me. Then there was silence. Then I heard a slithering sound as if something scaly was being dragged along, and a clacking on the wooden floorboards as if she was wearing high-heeled shoes.

I forced the sounds from my head. I had to keep going. Sweat was starting to prickle on my forehead and hands making my grip slippery as I held onto the stone and the door knocker.

Now I was certain I could hear breathing from very close by; breathing that wasn't mine.

I gave one frantic, final wrench and staggered backward as the disguised glass slipper snapped free into my hand. I hoped I hadn't broken it, but I was off and running before I could check. By the time I heard the door opening and a wail of pure fury from Latrina Earwax, I was already down the road and sprinting for cover as fast as I could.

I had done it. I had the first of the glass slippers in my hand and I had escaped from the strange Old Woman Who Lives in a Shoe.

I was elated. I couldn't believe how easy it had been.

I sprinted faster and whooped in triumph, unaware then of her terrifying secret—or of how she would take her horrifying revenge for my cheek.

CHAPTER
32

There was a wide passage which opened from the ledge cave that led down into the mountain. The lair had been guarded on their first visit but the goblins believed that no-one would dare to attack them now that the Beast was so powerful. Olive peeped into the cave and called out, "Hello? Anyone there?"

There was no answer at first, except an echo of her own voice, then they heard a slapping sound as a creature with broad, flat feet walked across a stone floor.

"Whozzat?" said an ugly, blue-skinned creature. It wore a leather skirt slung around its waist, and a belt from which hung a vicious-looking sword. A leather waistcoat completed its outfit. It had a long, hooked nose, almost no hair, and large, pointed ears. Its skin was blue and its eyes and teeth were yellow. It didn't look like the kind of creature who would enjoy pleasant chit-chat so Olive got straight to the point.

"I am Goldilocks and this is my trained dancing bear. We wish to perform for your king," she said without pausing for breath. She was so scared she didn't dare think. She hoped and hoped they would not recognize her.

"And get paid for it, don't forget," whispered Rory from behind her.

"And get paid for it," repeated Olive. The goblin spat on the ground near her feet but she willed herself not to look at it. She just hoped it wasn't green.

"Wait," said the goblin and disappeared back into the cave.

"What's going to happen now?" asked Rory.

"As soon as they come back for us, we'll go in. You start to dance and I'll sneak off to get the glass slipper. Keep dancing till I get back." Rory didn't answer. Olive guessed he was as scared as her.

"It'll be OK," she told him, and stroked his head. "You're a great dancer and I'm a great sneaker," she said.

He nodded.

"That's what my sister says about you too," he told her.

After a little while, the goblin returned. This time he had a friend with him, and they both carried sharp sticks. They pointed them at Rory.

"G'won then," they said. Olive worked out that this meant "go on then", so she walked into the dark cave, pausing for a minute to let her eyes adjust to the dimness. She heard a yelp of pain from behind her and whirled around to see one of the goblins poking his stick at Rory.

"Hey stop that," she said, furious. "How dare you hurt my bear." She clenched her fists and gritted her teeth as she stared at the goblin.

"Why? It's just a dumb animal," sneered the goblin. "Needs to be kept in its place."

"No it isn't," Olive shouted. "It's a living creature, and if you hurt it again, I'll take that stick of yours and I'll …"

Her threat remained unfinished as they were interrupted by two little goblin children. When they had been held captive by the goblins on their first visit to Dralfynia, she had noticed how cruel the goblin children were to each other, and they were no different on this second visit. They ran round and round each other, tripping one another up and pinching one another's ears. Whenever they caused pain, they laughed.

"Oi," shouted the first goblin. "Big Gob and Little Gob, pack it in. You know yer dad doesn't like yer coming out here. It's dangerous out in the world with all them disgusting pink humans and all that soap." At the mention of the word soap, the little goblins fled back up the corridor.

The moment of confrontation had passed. In sullen silence, the two goblins lead Rory and Olive along until they were in the vast underground chamber that belonged to the Goblin King, Azul.

He was seated on his throne in the middle of the cavern, watching them as they entered. His two sons had run to him after hearing about soap, and now they played around his feet. They had found a sharp stone and were poking his enormous toes with it. He gave a sudden roar of irritation and swiped them both away as if they were nothing more than flies.

Olive and Rory looked at each other. It was show time, and what an audience.

CHAPTER
33

"That was a piece of cake," I said, showing the brass-painted glass slipper to Aidan and Persis when I caught up with them. "So easy," I explained, seeing the puzzled look in Aidan's face. "That woman didn't even have a clue what was going on."

Now we had been successful at getting the slipper, it was time to carry out the next part of our plan. We hurried back to Tylwyth Teg, buzzing and chattering with the thrill of our first victory. Aidan's mom, Jill, had agreed to let us use their donkey cart for the journey to Timaru. She wasn't pleased about it though, Aidan told us. She didn't think it was good enough for Prince Charming and Sleeping Beauty. He had explained that we were hiding from the Beast and she changed her mind from 'no' to 'yes' straight away. When we got back to the Inn of the Fluffy Kitten, the donkey cart, complete with donkey, was standing ready for us. It was loaded with food and stone bottles of cool water.

I took the chance to run the glass slipper under the same pump I had used to wash Rory that morning. The brass-colored paint rinsed right off, leaving a beautifully carved and sparkling shoe. It glinted in the sunshine as I turned it around in my hand admiring the gleaming glass.

As I did so, a shadow fell over me. Something like a huge bird flew overhead but it was so high and so fast that it had disappeared by the time I looked up. It made me nervous, and the horse in the stable must have been unsettled too. It whinnied loudly. I hurriedly wrapped the slipper in a rag, then another one, and then another one. I slipped it into a canvas bag with a drawstring and slung it across my body. It would be safe there.

The cart was made from rough timber, and had two huge, solid wooden wheels. It was just big enough for Persis and me to sit in the back and for Aidan to sit on a bench at the front. He made sure that the donkey was happy to take us by asking it. We watched as the donkey nodded his head.

"We'll head for the next small village, Keeleton, and then this donkey will be rested there and we'll exchange her for another one," he explained. "That way we can keep going all night long and be in Timaru before dawn."

We nodded. We were just happy not to be walking this time, even though we had absolutely no idea where we were.

The afternoon slid by into evening. We clopped along through pretty countryside and then through a wood full of golden and scarlet leaves, and dappled sunshine.

"We're on the edge of Scary Forest," Aidan told us. We both shot up and bumped heads. "But it's not the scary part," he added—a little too late—as we rubbed our heads. "It takes a bit longer this way, but it's too dangerous to go through the black heart of the forest anymore." I wondered if this was something else we had caused. Witchy Wu's cottage was there, and perhaps her toxic fury toward us had poisoned the soul of the forest itself.

"Wood you believe it," a voice bellowed from nearby, but a little deeper into the forest. I rolled my eyes. Terrible puns on a tree theme? It could only be Rory's friend, Russell the talking tree. Russell's leaves rustled as he inched nearer to us. He stood on the side of the path we were following. Aidan drew the cart to a halt. We didn't have much time, but we definitely had enough time to talk to the tree that had saved Rory's life.

"And where is my little buddy, Rory?" asked Russell in his scratchy, rough voice. "I hope he hasn't varnished from sight?" I decided his puns had gotten worse since we last saw him. I filled Russell in on what was happening.

"Then I have some information to help you," he rumbled. "There is a were-dragon looking for you. She is a friend of Witchy Wu, and the wind tells me that you have something of hers."

"A were-dragon?" asked Persis, her voice trembling. "Is that what I think it is?"

It was Aidan who answered. "If you think it's someone who turns into a dragon at will and is strongest at the full moon, then yes, it's what you think it is. I thought they were a myth, but now I think I know what's been stealing our sheep."

CHAPTER
34

"They're not as bad as full dragons," said Russell helpfully. I think he saw Persis and me starting to freak out. "They are smaller and are only dangerous one week a month. Although," he carried on, "they are very fast and extremely cruel. And they hold a grudge forever," he finished. "Or should that be 'fir-ever'?" he chuckled.

"But what do we have that a were-dragon could possibly want?" Persis wanted to know. "I mean, we've never even seen a were-dragon."

I listened to her and then I thought back to just a few hours before. I thought back to a woman with leathery skin and a dress that shimmered gold and green. A woman with lifeless, green eyes. Worse than that, I thought back to the slithering sound I had heard on the other side of the door, and the clacking of what I had thought were high heels. That could also have been the sounds of a tail dragging across a wooden floor and talons scraping as a creature walked along—just inches from where I was stealing her prized possession.

I thought about being sick, but I managed to hold it together.

"I think," I said in a very tiny voice, because I didn't want to admit what I thought. "I think that the were-dragon is the Old Woman Who

Lives in a Shoe." Then I said, "And I think that what we have is one of her shoes." Unconsciously, I put a hand on the canvas sack that was slung across me. "Plus, I think that she flew overhead as I was washing the slipper at the Inn of the Fluffy Kitten."

Aidan swung around from the bench at the front of the cart and questioned me anxiously. I told him about the shadow and he sat gnawing at the side of one of his thumbs. I liked him, he made me feel braver and I wanted him to come to Timaru with Persis and me, but he had something else to do that mattered more.

"You have to go home and check on your family and the inn, don't you?" He didn't answer me, but I pushed on. "Persis and I don't really need you. We think you will only slow us down," I said. "Don't we Persis?" I added, poking at her ribs. She glared at me and rubbed her sore side, but she read my mind the way your very best friend does.

"Yeah," she agreed. "And we totally love walking in Scary Forest because it's good exercise," she added. It was a bit lame, but it did the trick.

"I'd hate to stop you two getting your daily exercise," said Aidan. We all knew that we were making up silly excuses, but it meant that Aidan could abandon us to protect his home without feeling too bad about it. I jumped out of the donkey cart. Persis clambered out more slowly, yawning loudly the whole time. We went and patted the donkey to say thanks for bringing us this far, and watched sadly as Aidan started to turn the donkey cart around.

It took a long time. In a car back in Melas, it would have taken my dad a few seconds as he went forward, backward, forward, and then off in the opposite direction. Aidan went forward, backward, forward, backward, forward, backward, forward, backward, forward, backward and finally forward again.

"Shall we just go?" Persis whispered after a few minutes. "This must be kind of embarrassing for him."

"And it is pretty boring," I agreed. I cleared my throat and went to Aidan.

"I hope your family and Twinkle are OK," I said. "And thanks for everything. Again." He flicked the reins to make the donkey shuffle forward an inch. "We promise to go rescue your friend, too," I said. He nodded.

"If I can, I'll come to Timaru later," he said. "It depends on what I find when I get back to Tylwyth Teg."

We waved at him and with heavy hearts we began our own journey in the opposite direction. Russell walked alongside us for a short way, asking questions about the Beast and Witchy Wu, and what was happening outside of Scary Forest. We told him what we had learned from Aidan.

"He thinks a war is coming?" asked Russell. "I know that the Beast and his allies are stronger than ever, but I did not know there was anyone on the other side to fight them."

"I guess it's the people themselves," I said. "They don't want their lives to be miserable under the Beast, so they are going to stand up to him."

"I hope they know what they are doing," said Russell.

CHAPTER
35

Olive was horrified. She had told the Goblin King that they were there to entertain him and the other goblins and they had watched Rory jig up and down a little, as a preview of his forthcoming attractions. Then Azul had told her that dancing was silly with no music and that she had to sing.

Sing.

In public.

Sing, in public, out loud, with no one else singing at the same time, in front of people, when she had never hit the right note once in her entire life.

She could feel Rory's eyes on her. If she stayed and sang (sorry, "sang"), then she would not be able to go get the glass slipper. On the other hand, if she didn't stay, then the goblins would get angry. She looked around her wildly, hoping to find some inspiration. Instead all she saw were black eyes staring at her and a cave so full of dirt and mess and junk that she could hardly see the floor.

And that's when inspiration came. It was a long shot, and it was risky—and there was no guarantee she was right. When she had been

Cinderella, she had needed to tidy up the room they were thrown into because it was such a mess. She just had to hope that the goblins hadn't bothered to clean up their home since.

As her mind worked out her crazy plan, there was no room for her to be creative. To buy some time while she thought, she had to sing. Unfortunately, because everyone was staring at her, she couldn't think of a single song.

Rory gave an encouraging little growl. Then she thought of the one song that she could sing that even she couldn't ruin.

"Happy birthday to you," she began. Rory's forehead wrinkled. How as he supposed to dance to that?

"Happy birthday to you," she continued. He hopped from one foot to the other.

"Happy birthday dear evil-goblin-kingggg," she warbled. Rory turned around in a circle.

"Happy birthday to you," she finished with a flourish. Rory dropped to one knee and flung his front paws out wide.

Ta-daa. They had performed.

It was terrible. But Olive's plan worked. Before they could say "Do you want an encore?" they were being dragged away and thrown into the same cave as they had been thrown into before. There had been booing and jeering and some goblins had thrown things at them, but they had made it. A goblin stood on guard outside the cave with his back was to them. Rory took a minute to work out what had happened.

"Was that your plan then?" he whispered.

"What do you mean?"

"To pretend to sing so badly that I couldn't dance, and then we'd be thrown in here to find the glass slipper?"

"Sure, that was my plan all along," Olive told him. "I just pretended to sing really badly." She ran her hand along a rocky shelf as she spoke until she found what she was looking for. The last time they were in the cave, she had placed a few pretty things on the shelf while she was making their prison-cave more homely. Her fingers closed on a smooth, cool object, with another right next to it. Carefully she lifted them down. She held a glittering glass slipper which matched the one that Sabrina now had, but Olive's one had the heel snapped off. She held the heel in her other hand and looked at it. There was a dark brown stain on it and it was savagely sharp. She remembered Aidan telling them that when the prince and his sister Princess Heidi had quarrelled many years ago, he had tried to take the glass slipper from her. The heel of the slipper had snapped off, severing the first of the Beast's missing fingers.

Eeoowww. That brown stain must be the Beast's blood. Gross. She didn't want to touch it anymore, so she looked for something soft to place it on where it would be safe.

Rory was on all four feet keeping watch on the goblin. She put the slipper and its broken heel on Rory's furry back, then stepped back quickly as blue sparks shot out.

CHAPTER
36

A smell of burning hair filled the cave and a plume of smoke rose from the middle of Rory's back. Rory gave a little yawn.

Shocked, Olive snatched the glass slipper back and started patting out the smoldering fur.

"What are you doing?" Rory said crossly, trying to twist his neck far enough to see over his shoulder.

"Nothing," said Olive, trying to blow out the last embers.

"Why are you blowing on my back?" Rory hissed at her.

"You were on fire for a few seconds there, but it's OK now," she told him.

"You set me on fire?" Rory was astonished.

"It was by mistake," said Olive, "and you sure have really thick fur. You never even felt it. Which is a good thing," she added, making her voice bright and casual. She hoped he would never be able to see the round, scorched shape in the middle of his back and that the fur would grow back fast.

"What happened?" Rory asked, his voice getting a little louder now.

"Shush," she said. "I just put the glass slipper on your back so that it wouldn't go on the ground and maybe break," she continued. Rory interrupted her.

"You were using me as a shelf?"

"Um, well, yes. But then some sparks came out of the slipper as soon as it touched you and ..." She stopped and looked down. The slipper was fixed. There was no brown stain, no separate heel. It was a complete and perfect glass slipper. Somehow, the fire on Rory's back—or maybe Rory himself—had repaired it.

She walked around to the front of Rory and held the mended slipper out to him so he could see it. He sniffed it and shrugged. He'd smelled more interesting things in his time as Baby Bear.

"Now what?" he wanted to know. The goblin who had been guarding their cave suddenly blocked the doorway as he stood there, casting dark shadows all around the room.

"Woss going in in there?" he said. "Ooo you talkin' to?" he demanded of Olive. She thought fast. The time they had left before being sucked back to Melas was ticking away and they needed to be heading to Timaru as soon as they could.

"I was practicing my singing," she said. "Please go tell King Azul that my bear and I are ready for the real performance now. And this time it will be fantastic." She couldn't tell if the goblin believed her or not but he turned away and she heard him heading along the narrow corridor that joined their cave to the main cavern.

"Come on," she said to Rory. "We have to go now."

"What? Where?"

"The same way we escaped last time," Olive said. "My guess is that these goblins are such lazy housekeepers, Sabrina's hair will still be there to help us down the mountainside."

This seemed like a wild hope more than a well-constructed plan to Rory, but Olive was already shoving the glass slipper into a pocket of her white frilly apron as she peeked into the passageway.

"All clear," she announced then she reached back and ripped some fur from Rory's shoulder. Ignoring the yelp of irritation that he gave, she used it to pad the glass slipper. She hoped it would be enough to keep it safe on their journey. Then, beckoning Rory to follow her, she hurried in the opposite direction that the goblin had taken until she reached a slit at the end of the passage. It was supposed to act as a window but she planned to use it as their escape route.

Sure enough, a thick, very long hank of yellow hair hung limply from the window. One end of it was trapped under a rock inside the cave; the other had been thrown out and down the steep, rocky mountainside. When they escaped last time, they had needed to cut off Sabrina's hair close to her scalp— Olive hoped that it was still there so she and Rory would be able to use it as a rope to climb down.

"Thank goodness goblins are such slobs," thought Olive. Rory had joined her. He didn't look happy.

"How will I fit through that window?" he asked. "And how will I hold onto Rapunzel's hair?" He held up his paws. "Look, no fingers and thumbs." He sounded scared, and Olive felt terrible. She hadn't even thought about Rory being Baby Bear and the problems it would bring.

"I'll lift you up to the window and push you through from this side," she said. "And after that, you'll just have to use your claws to dig into the hair and kind of slide down. It'll be fun," she told him.

It wasn't.

CHAPTER
37

Rory stood on his hind legs and placed his front paws onto the window ledge. Olive stood behind him, squatted down and rested her cheek against his haunch. She locked the fingers of both hands together so that she made a kind of step with her hands and Rory put one back foot on it then pushed himself up. His sharp claws dug into her palms making them bleed and his rear end was worryingly near to her face.

As he scrabbled up, he used her hands, then her shoulders and then her face as steps until he was on the ledge. He turned sideways and got one shoulder out. Before he forced his head through the narrow gap, he looked at her.

"Hey, Olive?"

"Yes?"

"Bet you're glad I didn't ask you to pull my claw," he said, a smirk on his furry face.

Olive raised a hand to her face to push away some hair that had come loose and realized that Rory's feet had scratched her forehead badly. She hoped she would not have a scar. Cute as he was, Rory was being a royal pain. And, to cap it all, he was now stuck. Taking a deep breath, Olive pushed against Rory's body with all her might. Nothing happened. She leaned her shoulder onto Rory and shoved with her feet, straining all her muscles, until there was a sudden pop and Rory was tumbling through the window and down the steep slope. All she could do was watch in fascinated dismay as he curled into a ball and rolled down the mountain, bouncing from rock to rock until he reached the bottom. He lay perfectly still for a frightening few seconds. Then he got to his four feet and shook himself from nose to rear.

She didn't have time to wonder at his luck; she could hear voices coming her way so she leaped to the ledge and crawled through. Her own progress was much slower than Rory's. She wasn't athletic like Sabrina and Persis and several times she almost fell. She could hardly manage to support her own weight with her arms and soon they were aching and trembling. The hair was cutting into her already sore palms and it became slippery with her blood. Time after time she stubbed her toes or slipped and missed her footing, scraping her shins on sharp rocks.

From behind her she heard Rory's voice.

"What?" she yelled back.

"Olive, they're up in the window. I think they see you," he called up to her. Oh no. She didn't dare look up. It would make her even more frightened and she might not be able to carry on moving. She kept taking it one step at a time, trying to breathe deeply to keep calm. Then she felt a tugging on the hair. Her eyes filled with tears.

"Please, please don't let them start to follow me down," she whispered taking another step. There was another sharp tug and then she felt herself pulled back an inch up the mountainside.

No! This time, instead of following them, the goblins were going to pull her back up. And all because she couldn't sing? It didn't seem fair. She risked a glance upwards and saw three pairs of shiny, yellow eyes looking down at her. She began to cry openly. She thought that her arms would be ripped from their sockets if she dangled there much longer.

Yank. Up she went another inch. Her toes banged against the stones, sending a shower of pebbles down the mountainside.

She heard Rory's voice again. It was much closer this time.

"Olive? Olive!" Twisting her neck, she could manage to look down over her shoulder to the ground that was still so far below her. To her astonishment, Rory was floating along nearby.

"Jump," he told her. "Ruggy and I will catch you."

She whimpered. She would never manage to do that. Just jump? And trust a talking bear and a flying carpet that kept trying to bounce her off? No way.

"Jump!" Rory was screaming at her now. In the end, she didn't have the courage to jump but the pain of holding on and the slipperiness of her grasp on the hair were too much. She felt her grip give way, closed her eyes and started to fall, screaming all the way.

Whumpff! She landed on something soft and furry. Something that complained a lot about what a big lump she was. She opened one eye then the other.

"Next time, keep your eyes open and you'll land on Ruggy, not me," said Rory, shoving her off him. Carefully she sat up, checking herself over. She was sore and her arms and back ached. She had several cuts and scrapes, but nothing was broken and she was alive. She and Rory floated high above the ground on Ruggy.

She flung her arms around Rory's neck and hugged him tightly.

"Stop it," came his muffled voice. "You're a girl and I hate girls because you all smell funny."

CHAPTER
38

We hadn't arranged a particular place to meet in Timaru, so Persis and I waited by the well where we had cast a magic spell and returned home to Melas the last time. It was really the only place we all knew. We hoped that Rory and Olive would arrive soon. Time was trickling away.

"I hope that the were-dragon didn't go to Aidan's place and cause any damage," Persis said. I was silent. I hoped so too. I couldn't believe how many problems our previous visit to Dralfynia had caused. I felt restless. I took out the glass slipper from my bag and rubbed it with my sleeve to make it shine even more. I held it up to the early morning sun and watched it send rainbows chasing across the ground. We had been slouching on the grass, our backs against the wooden boards that surrounded the well. I stirred and stood up.

"Shall we go explore for a while?" I suggested. Persis shook her head.

"No thanks; I need a nap," she said. "That was a really long walk, almost right through the night," she said. "I need my beauty sleep." She firmly closed her eyes and settled down. I left her and began to wander through the narrow, cobbled streets of Timaru. It was busy at the start of the working day, and people were hurrying about their business. I saw windows that were filled with differently shaped loaves of bread and another one full of jars of honey and jam. Occasionally, I saw signs saying how much things cost and saw them being bought by people in fancy clothes. I could see that Timaru was a lot different to Tylwyth Teg.

As I wandered around, I began to notice a few people staring at me, and three times, people bowed as I passed them. After a few minutes, I realized that a small group of people were behind me, following me. I turned around and looked at them. They were all girls. I smiled at them, wondering what was going on. They immediately dropped into low curtseys.

Then things got even stranger. Two women swooped out of the front door of a large house and chased the others away, shaking their large fists at them. I took the opportunity to start scurrying off, trying to find my route back to Persis. This was starting to unsettle me.

"Not so fast, Your Highness," came a deep voice. A large, hairy hand clamped down on my shoulder. It wore a lace glove and thick hairs poked through the holes in the lace. My eyes followed the hand all the way up a muscular arm covered in a pink fabric patterned with little bunches of flowers, to a face that was covered with heavy makeup and topped with an intricate wig full of little bows and curls. The face smiled at me, showing very few teeth. I let my gaze travel beyond her. There was another person standing next to her. This one grinned at me as well and also showed me a lot of gum. My eyes flicked from one grinning face to the other. They looked very similar. They must be related. They must be brothers? No … they were sisters.

Oh! They were those sisters.

They were looking at me like a starving person looks at food.

"Hi," I said, because I couldn't think of anything else to say.

"Ooooo, he spoke to us," they giggled and cooed at each other.

"Are you here to visit Prince Donaldo? He's moved into the castle to look after his Aunty Yvonne," one of them said.

Me? Visit the prince?

They sat on the ground and began to unlace their boots. Finally, the penny dropped. They thought I was the real Prince Charming and they wanted to try on the glass slipper, which I still held in my hand.

"Oh no, wait," I said, flapping my hand at them. "You've made a mistake. I'm not really Prince Charming."

"Yes you are," said one of them. She sounded much less friendly all of a sudden. I plowed on anyway.

"And this isn't the real glass slipper," I said, thinking of the one that I hoped Rory and Olive were collecting.

"Yes it is," said the other one. She didn't sound very friendly anymore either.

I had no idea what to do. They were bigger and stronger than me, and they were very focused. One minute they were standing there smiling, the next they had their boots and stockings off and were barefoot and tapping their feet.

I just decided to go with it. I mean, how many weird things can happen to a girl in a day? Apparently quite a few, I was starting to realize. I knelt down and placed the tiny, delicate glass slipper on the huge big toe of one of the Sisters.

CHAPTER
39

"What are you doing?" said Olive's voice from behind me. Blushing scarlet, I jumped up.

"These ladies wanted to try on the glass slipper," I said, as if it was completely normal. Olive rolled her eyes, shook her head and grabbed my arm.

"Come on," she said. "We've got a girl to rescue and a trip to the Island of Merthyr before dawn, remember?"

"Hang on a minute, lassie," said the Sister who had not yet tried on the slipper. "I don't know who you think you are, but it's my turn to try that on." Her voice was almost a snarl and she snatched the delicate glass slipper from my fingers.

Olive and I gasped, certain that she would break it as she tried to force her foot into the glass slipper.

"Something wrong with it," she said. She pulled her foot out, leaving some skin and what looked like a verruca behind. I wrinkled my nose in disgust as she handed it back to me.

"It's not even comfy, you know what I mean?" she continued. "How could you go dancing in that?" She had a point. I had never wondered that before. I gave a weak laugh, and then I remembered who their step-sister was.

"I say, my good women," I said. Olive gave a snort of laughter. I ignored her. If they believed I was a prince then I had to act like a prince and this was the best I could do.

"I say, perhaps you two gorgeous girls can help me. I'm looking for someone, a poor servant girl," I said.

"It'd better not be that Ellie," said the first Sister. "Because if it is …" She shook her very large fist in the air and twisted her mouth into a gummy snarl.

"No, no, no," I said. "Ha, ha. No. Definitely not anyone called 'Ellie'. But just supposing it was her, where would I find her?"

"Well, seeing as it isn't actually her, then it's OK to tell you," said the second Sister. I was getting a headache. This was too complicated.

"If it was her, but it isn't, she'd be up in that tower, the one right at the back of the Royal Castle. And best place for her, too," she added, spitting on the ground. "Prince Donaldo said she helped some wicked criminals escape so he locked her up," she said. Her sister nodded.

"And what's more, she's always stealing our princes, she is. Showing up at parties and talking to pumpkins. She's a bit you know, cuckoo," she added, twirling her index finger in a circle level with her forehead.

"Right, well thanks very much for your help and good luck finding a prince that isn't me," I said. Olive and I began to slowly back away, and then turned. As soon as we were out of sight, we ran back to the well and to the others.

I was so relieved to see Olive, Rory and Ruggy—and to find out that they had the other glass slipper—that I forgot all about being annoyed with Olive for talking to Bridget. We swapped our stories and then wished we hadn't.

"So now we have a were-dragon to add to our list of people who want to capture us?" said Olive. I nodded. Persis held out her hands to us, wanting the glass slippers. We gave them to her and she put them on the ground, next to each other.

"They're so pretty," she admitted. "But I don't see what all the fuss is about. I mean, with Ruggy, he's a magic flying carpet. These are just a pair of shoes." Before I could stop her, she took off her own shoes and put on the glass slippers.

"Yeouwch," she said. "These are the most uncomfortable shoes ever," and she pulled them off again quickly. "Give me a pair of sneakers any day." I wondered whether to tell her that one of the Sisters' verrucas was now stuck to her foot.

I decided to keep quiet.

Then Olive wanted to have a go. She took her apron and wiped the shoes inside and out first. Like Persis, her feet were small enough to cram in, if you ignored the bent toes and the bleeding heels. She stood up in them and wobbled.

"I see what you mean," she said to Persis. "They really hurt, don't they?" She tried a few steps. As the most fashion-conscious of us, she would be the one most likely to suffer for her style but even she gave up quickly. "They're too tight at the toes and the glass edges really cut into your feet," she complained. She sat on the grass, took off the glass slippers and began to rub her feet.

Now I wanted a go as well. I undid the buckles and laces on my sneakers and pulled them off. I slid my feet into the slippers and walked forward. I wasn't used to wearing heels so I teetered a bit at first, but I didn't know what all the fuss was about. They were really comfortable and they fitted perfectly. I tried jogging a few paces and even did a little jump.

Then I heard Rory say, "Hey, where'd Sabrina go?"

"I'm right here," I said. I was surprised when they all screamed.

CHAPTER 40

Aidan saw the black smoke rising from Tylwyth Teg long before he was close enough to see the village itself. He was leading the tired donkey by now and helping pull the cart, but when he saw the dark cloud coil like a snake into the sky, he let go of the reins and began to run.

Aware that the donkey would follow him home at her own pace, Aidan's legs pumped as he forced himself onward. His heart thudded wildly in his chest and whenever he breathed, he dragged smutty air into his lungs. His parents! His home! Twinkle and his other friends! Oh no, the secret he had hidden in the stables! As he ran closer, he felt the heat touch his skin and swamp him.

A crowd of villagers had gathered, blocking the way through to his home. As he drew closer, he saw that they had formed a human chain and were passing buckets of water from the pump in the yard through to the fire.

From where he was watching, Aidan could see an orange glow that lit the evening sky and seemed to be coming from where the inn stood. Scarlet and yellow flames licked at the clouds and sparks fizzed into the air, threatening nearby buildings.

Aidan's knees felt so weak he could hardly stand and the smoke was so dense it was hard to make out people's faces. He started to push through the crowd to get as close to the Inn of the Fluffy Kitten as he could. One man objected to the boy shoving him out of the way. He turned angrily, ready to argue, until he saw who it was.

"Make way! Let him through," he called out. "Aidan's back. Let him get to the front." Grateful for the help, Aidan forced his way from one end of the crowd to the other and quickly reached the front. He couldn't believe that so many of the people of Tylwyth Teg had come to help. They had soaked the dry thatch of the inn itself. Water dripped to the ground and the hard earth was muddy. Twinkle sat in her sign, her fur soaked and stuck to her skin, and a very sulky expression on her face.

At the very front of the crowd, Aidan saw his mom. She was taking buckets full of water from the person behind her and throwing it over the burning toilet building, then passing the empty bucket to someone else who sent it back on its way to be refilled. The inn was safe but the bathroom was a ruin.

Aidan touched her arm.

"Mom," he said. She scooped him into a quick hug, then handed him a full bucket.

"I need a break, son," she said. "My arms are so tired." He nodded and took her place in the line. As he threw the water up as high as he could onto the roof, he shouted questions to her.

"Where's Dad? And Jack?" Almost all the men in Tylwyth Teg were called Jack, including his cousins and brother.

"They're soaking the roofs of the other buildings in the village," she told him. "We didn't want the fire to spread."

"So no one's hurt?"

"No, we're all OK," she said. The relief he felt turned his arms and legs to jelly for a moment and he almost dropped his bucket. Not wanting to show his emotion in front of everyone else in the village, he carried on working and asking questions at the same time.

"What happened?" Then he answered his own question. "It was it a dragon, wasn't it?" His mother stood back up and took the empty bucket from his hand. She gave it to someone else in the line, telling them to take over. The fire was almost out by now and her son had some questions to answer.

"How did you know that, Aidan?" He scratched his ear while he thought, then his words came out in a big rush.

"Because Mrs. Earwax, from the shoe museum, is a were-dragon. I think she's the one who's been stealing a sheep from us every month. Today, those girls I was with took a magic glass slipper from her so that they could give it to Queen Hazel and King Michael to look after and keep safe from the Beast. One of the girls was washing the shoe here afterward, and the were-dragon flew overhead and saw her. As soon as I found out, I rushed back to help." He looked at her, waiting for her to be angry. Her bathroom had just been burned to the ground by a dragon after all.

"Girls?" she said "I thought one was a boy."

CHAPTER 41

"Stop screaming," I said, irritated. I didn't know what was up with them all. "We don't want to draw attention to ourselves." I looked around to see if any of the townspeople were looking our way, but apart from an idle glance or two, they were busy with their own business.

"If you didn't want to draw attention to us then you shouldn't be playing tricks on us," Persis said. "Where are you hiding?"

"I'm not hiding," I told her. They were really annoying me—this was obviously a very silly practical joke. "I'm standing right here." Persis got to her feet, stretched out her arms and started to walk slowly around, as if she had her eyes closed, like when we played "Marco Polo."

Then she pushed me over. One minute I was standing there, the next she swung round, her arms smacked into me and I fell down. The really unfair thing was that she was the one who yelped out in surprise—I mean, I get knocked down and she cries out?

Then she took a step and fell over my leg, landing right on top of me.

"Ooooof! Get off me," I said, trying to wriggle free from her. Every time I moved an arm or leg, she did too and we stayed there for a couple of minutes, me trying to get free and Persis blocking me. We rolled over one another in the grass by the well and we were in real danger of rolling down the gentle slope that led from the well to the main streets of Timaru.

"What are you doing?" I grunted, giving her a shove. "Can't you see that I'm trying to get up?"

"No," she gasped. "We can't see you at all. We can only hear you." Then she used my stomach as leverage to haul herself back onto her feet and stood there, panting. She flicked her hair from her face then turned to a patch of daisies and started talking to them.

"When you tried on the glass slippers," she said, "you disappeared." I looked down at myself. She was right. Instead of seeing my legs, my fancy pink prince-jacket and my hands and feet, I saw grass. It was like looking through an empty drinking glass. I could see through my legs but everything was a bit distorted.

Hey, this was cool.

"Just a minute," I said. I'd had an idea. "I'll take the slippers off and see what happens." Then I sneaked around as quietly as I could until I was standing right behind Rory.

"Yarrrr!" I yelled, then collapsed to the ground, laughing so hard I got a stitch in my side. He had been so shocked that he jumped right off the ground; then he had tried to swipe at the air where I had been standing but missed and fell over.

Eventually, I wiped the tears from my eyes, sat up and kicked at one of the slippers with the other to knock it free. Being invisible had its advantages, but my fun couldn't last forever.

The slipper was a snug fit and wouldn't come off easily. I bent my knee so that my foot was pulled closer to me, took the slipper in both hands, and tried wrestle it off. Nothing happened, except that my hands slipped and I smacked my own nose by mistake.

"Guys, I can't get them off," I said. I was starting to panic.

"Lie on your back with your legs in the air," Persis instructed me. "Then keep talking so we can follow your voice and find you." I did as she told me.

"Um well, I can't really think of anything to say, so I'll just say some random words and—ow, that's my arm," I said. The next thing I knew, Olive had hold of one of the slippers and Persis had the other. They stood over me and wriggled and wiggled and wrenched and pushed and pulled. Rory had his back to me. He was still sulking because I had given him a scare, so he refused to help.

"Maybe we need some butter," suggested Persis. "To make it easier to slip them off."

"Or something to use as a shoe horn and force her feet out," said Olive.

"Why don't you just press the bows?" said a different voice. We all looked over.

We saw Aidan. He was sitting on Clyde.

CHAPTER 42

"Clyde! How did you get here?"

"What happened? Is everything OK in Tylwyth Teg?"

"Are Twinkle and your family OK?

Persis, Rory and Olive all spoke at once and rushed over to see them both. It took a couple of minutes for me to find and press the bows on my glass slippers. I heard a little "snick" sound as I touched each one, and when I tried again to remove the slippers, they came off easily.

I looked down. I could see myself again. I tugged on my sneakers—much better. I padded over to the others and laid my head on Clyde's neck. I breathed in deeply. He smelled of horse and home to me. Just being with him made me feel calmer. I stroked him and looked into his eyes. I couldn't believe he was with us in Dralfynia again.

"I'm happy you're here," I told him. Then I looked up at Aidan. "And you," I added. "But I'm surprised to see you so soon."

Aidan told us all about getting back to Tylwyth Teg to find that the were-dragon had tried to set fire to his inn, but instead had destroyed only the bathrooms. My hand flew to my mouth. I had hoped that the rumors we heard from Russell weren't true—but here I was again, feeling terrible because my attempt to help had led to terrible consequences. Aidan saw the expression on my face.

"It's OK," he said to me. "Nobody was hurt and my mom's been asking my dad for an indoor bathroom for years, so now she'll get what she wants." I didn't feel any better, but it was nice of him to try and make me feel less guilty.

"Your Hi— I mean Sabrina," he said. "You must understand that anything you do that helps us stand up to the Beast with Eight Fingers is good. At least we know now that Latrina Earwax is our enemy—and what's been happening to our sheep." That was true. I felt a tiny bit better after all.

Clyde dipped his head down and Aidan slid from his back, surprised at the unexpected movement. Clyde suddenly had spotted the bear cub. He pawed at the ground with one of his front hooves and started to sniff Rory all over.

Poor Rory—or rather, poor Clyde.

I could tell that Rory wasn't sure what to do as Clyde's nose got deeper into his fur; Clyde began to huff and snuffle, as if he recognized that this was Rory and was saying hello. Then Clyde lifted his head and gave a gigantic sneeze. A plume of vapor came from each nostril and hung in the cold air. I laughed.

"You look like a dragon, Clyde," I told him. He whinnied and raised his horn proudly.

Olive asked Aidan what we all wanted to know. "So how did you manage to find Clyde and bring him here? The last time we saw him he was back home in his field." Aidan gave a shrug; he seemed surprised that we didn't know what had happened.

"I expect Bridget Bishop sent him to watch over you," he said. I thought about it. It seemed that my stepmom knew we had taken her potion and come to Dralfynia and although she hadn't come herself, as far as I knew, she had sent Clyde. Wow; this was a very impressive care package.

"You mean he just appeared in Tylwyth Teg?" I asked. Aidan nodded.

"Yes, he came with you. He's been here all along." We looked at each other. We looked at Aidan. We looked at Clyde.

"I thought you knew," Aidan said. "He's been in our stable back at the inn."

Then I remembered glimpsing a horse behind Nathan and Heath when they were distracting Witchy Wu back at school. I remembered hearing a horse several times in the stable and I remembered Aidan saying he already had some help with carrying the heavy pails of milk. Finally, I remembered a pair of ears peeping out from behind a giant pumpkin.

Good old Clyde. He really had been looking out for us all this time. And with everything that we still needed to get done, I suspected that we were going to need all the help we could get.

"I see you have the pair of glass slippers," said Aidan, nodding at them as they dangled from my hand. "Does that mean you are going to the Island of Merthyr to hide them and Ruggy?"

"Well, yes," I said. "But not yet. First we have to break into the tower at the back of the Royal Castle and get your friend out."

He grinned and clapped me hard on the back, the way boys do to each other.

Sigh.

CHAPTER
43

Our plan to rescue Ellie from the tower was the same as all our plans. Sneak in somewhere, make it up as we went along and escape at the last second with lots of drama and people chasing us. When I mentioned sneaking in, I noticed Olive glare at me, but I had no idea why.

For now, it was all about Persis. It was her turn to shine.

"Just act like a princess," I told her. "Be all grand and we'll be your followers. You distract the Beast by um, offering to trade your kingdom's crop of um, turnips for some pumpkins. I'll put on the slippers and find Ellie. Then ..." my voice trailed off.

"Then, you can roll her up in Ruggy and pretend that she's some luggage, put her on Clyde's back and we can all just casually walk out of the Royal Castle. No one will suspect a thing," Rory finished.

Of course. A group made up of a talking bear, a huge Clydesdale unicorn, a princess who was always napping, a girl with hair in loop-de-loop braids and a body-shaped rug with feet sticking out the end—no one would suspect a thing.

Unfortunately, and as usual, we couldn't come up with anything better.

"Parsnips and pumpkins?" Persis repeated, an edge in her voice. "I don't know anything about vegetables." She was right.

"Turnips," I corrected her. "Look, I can't think of everything," I said grumpily. "You'll be fine." She didn't look impressed.

We laid Ruggy across Clyde's back, shoved Persis up to sit on top of Ruggy and stood back to check out our work.

"The Beast will never fall for it," said Olive. Finding out he was living at the castle full-time had added another problem and she was right. Persis looked ridiculous and as soon as the Beast saw Ruggy, he'd know straight away what he was. Not to mention the fact that I would be there with the glass slippers in my bag. We would be walking into a whole heap of trouble. I sat down heavily on the grass and put my hands over my face. I gave a huge sigh.

"I don't know what to do," I moaned. I wished Dad was there to make it all OK. I was fed up of being a leader. I was fed up of being in Dralfynia. I was fed up of having to solve problems. I just wanted my dad.

"Oh Highness? Prince Charming?" trilled a deep voice that was trying to be perky. I separated my fingers and peeked out through the gap. That was all I needed. The Sisters were skipping over to see me. They had little lacy fans and were waving them in front of their faces then snapping them shut and smacking each other playfully with them. I slowly shook my head as I watched their approach through my fingers.

"Who are they?" asked Persis. The Sisters caught sight of Persis with her beautiful dress and long, shiny hair. She was perched side-saddle on Clyde's back. They did not look pleased to see her.

"Who are we?" they repeated. "Don't you mean who are you?"

"What? No, I know who I am," she said. Then Persis gave one of her huge yawns, so big it looked as though her head was going to split in two.

"Oh, it's youuuuuu," said one of the Sisters. She made the word "you" sound like a terrible insult.

"Come to look at the magic spinning wheel in our castle, have you?" said the other Sister.

"Worried it might be the magic spinning wheel that will send you to sleep for a hundred years?" sneered the first Sister.

Ah ha! If she wasn't interested in the spinning wheel before, she was now, I thought. I uncovered my face and jumped to my feet.

"Ladies," I said. They both gave little squeals and hid their faces behind their fans. Unfortunately, their heads were quite big and the fans were quite small. I could see traces of beard showing at the bottom.

Thanks to them, I'd had a brilliant idea—even better than the turnips one.

"You both look lovely today," I said as they bobbed down in a curtsey. "How would you like to come with us to the Royal Castle and meet the Beast—I mean the prince? I hear he is looking for a bride." I hauled them both up out of the curtseys that they had gotten stuck in. Then I spoke the magic words that I knew would send them into a spin. "He wants to make his bride a princess."

They both fell down in a dead faint.

It turned out that the Sisters weren't really very mean; they were just completely obsessed with marrying a prince.

CHAPTER
44

Sometime later, we were ready. The Sisters told us their names were Enid and Agatha, then they skipped back home to get changed, like a pair of jolly elephants. When they came back, they brought with them some very fancy ribbons and blankets which they used to decorate Clyde for us. Ruggy was well hidden underneath them all. Persis had climbed back up and we were finally ready to go.

I fretted about the wasted time. In Dralfynia, people didn't seem to worry about time, but for us it was running out. Without a phone or even a watch, I couldn't tell exactly how much time was left, but we had already been there almost two days and we needed to keep moving, as we would soon be leaving forever.

'Forever.' That had a nice sound to it.

Now that they had their best (i.e. most frilly) dresses on, Enid and Agatha were hustling us along as quickly as they could. We trotted through Timaru and began the walk up the craggy hill to the castle. As we drew closer, I could see that it was even more scruffy and unloved than it had been the last time we were there.

When we crossed the drawbridge, I peered over the side to the moat below. It was nothing more than a mud pit. If it had been in Melas, someone would have dumped a shopping trolley there. The planks that made up the drawbridge were worn and didn't fit together very well. It creaked like an old bed as we hurried over it.

On the other hand, the guards were in smart uniforms and had brand new spears, shields and swords. I knew this because a line of them stood at the entrance to the castle with their weapons drawn and pointing straight at us.

It was time to bluff.

"Step aside, peasants," I said. I sounded like a twelve-year-old girl, which is, of course, what I was. "It is me, I mean 'I', Prince Charming—and my BFF, I mean my friend, Princess Sleeping Beauty. She wishes to view the prince's spinning wheel." Enid scuttled up to whisper in my ear then scuttled back. "And my other friends, Enid and Agatha. We, uh, we …" This time Agatha scuttled up to whisper in my ear and then scuttled back. "We seek an audience with the prince," I repeated.

"The prince is busy," one of the guards said. Oh. I hadn't even thought that the prince wouldn't want to see visitors; I had been too busy worrying about what would happen when he did agree to see us.

I didn't have to try and think of excuses to get in, however. Enid and Agatha now rudely shoved past me and went straight up to the guards, their hands on their hips and their attitudes tuned to "don't mess with us."

The conversation did not take very long. The Sisters were a tornado and anything in their path just had to watch out. After a short argument followed by lots of apologizing, we were through.

We stood in a big courtyard with high walls to the left and right. There were walkways at the tops of the walls, along which more guards were pacing and watching to see who was coming toward the castle. Ahead of us was the door to the tower where Ellie was being held captive.

Enid and Agatha were a fantastic distraction. They noticed a door being guarded especially heavily and asked if that was where the prince was. They were told no, absolutely not, definitely no way, which they correctly interpreted as yes, absolutely so, definitely yes way. Aidan hurried over to make sure they were OK, but he needn't have bothered—all he could do was stand and watch as the Sisters surged toward that door, taking with them any guards who tried to stop them. By the time they had their hands on the door handle, they were dragging along with them six poor guards who had their hands clasped around Enid's and Agatha's ankles. It gave the rest of us the time we needed.

I yanked off my sneakers and thrust them into my pockets. Then I quickly pulled the slippers from my bag and slipped into them again. I looked down to make sure I really was invisible and was relieved to see cobblestones where my toes should have been—I'd have hated to stroll over to the tower then find that all the guards were staring at me!

Persis wriggled around until she finally managed to pull Ruggy out from underneath her. She rolled him up, tied him firmly with some of the leather string that had been crisscrossed around Aidan's legs, and then she passed him down to me. I took Ruggy and started across the courtyard.

"Brina, wait," hissed Persis. "We can't see you, but we can still see Ruggy."

CHAPTER 45

Oops. I quickly dropped poor Ruggy on the ground before someone saw a rolled-up mat floating in mid-air, although for all I knew, in Dralfynia that might be perfectly normal.

"What shall I do?" I whispered back.

"Just go get her," said Olive, irritated with all the delays. "We'll wait nearby and deal with it when you come back, but you'll have to hurry up. I don't know how long those Sisters are going to distract the guards and the Beast for." I flung up my hands in a gesture to show "yeah, OK, I'm going, don't nag me", but Olive didn't respond. There was a short silence, then she said, "Are you still here?" I rolled my eyes, told her that yes, I was still there, then scurried across to the tower.

I could still hear her grumbling at me as I started off.

I skirted around people as I crossed the courtyard, aware that even though they couldn't see me, they could feel me if I bumped into them and hear me if I sneezed or spoke. A cluster of people had gathered to watch the guards being dragged along the ground by Enid and Agatha and I needed to get past them. Then, from the side of me I heard a rumbling sound. A guard pushing a cart piled high with heavy coils of rope was heading straight toward me and I had nowhere to go.

I breathed in, put my head down and hoped. It felt wrong not to say "excuse me, please" as I squeezed through the small crowd, but this wasn't the time for courtesy. Instead, I gritted my teeth and hoped that none of the men and women I was pushing past would reach out and realize I was there. I pressed through a tiny gap between two people and then gently pushed another out of my way with my hand on her back.

"Hey, mind what you're doing," I heard someone say above my head.

"What do you mean?" someone else answered.

"I mean quit shoving me," said the first voice. Oh dear; I hoped I wasn't going to start a fight.

The rumbling from behind me grew louder.

"Coming through. Make way," called the guard with the cart. The people around me moved apart slightly. They were letting him through. I was the only thing standing in his way. I scuttled through the gap in the crowd, then realized that the only place for me to avoid being run over was a space between the cart and the wall around the courtyard. I pressed my back against the rough wall and waited for the man to go by.

As he came nearer, I flattened myself more into the wall. He seemed to be aiming straight for me. I squeezed my eyes closed, I didn't know what else to do.

"Yeowch." I couldn't help myself give a little squeak of pain. One of the wheels on the cart had rolled right over my foot, crushing the toes. I heard a crunching noise and thought the glass slippers would have shattered, but they seemed pretty tough. I put my finger in my mouth and bit gently down on it to take my mind off the pain coming from my poor toes.

Then I heard Olive's voice, still grumbling, drift across the yard.

"… and I haven't seen the tower door open, so she hasn't even gotten to the tower yet," she said. "What is she even doing?" Tempting as it was to go back and tell her about my "ouchy", I decided to be brave and limped over to the tower door.

"Hope you're happy now," I thought to myself as I twisted the circular black metal ring that should have opened the door, and pulled it to me.

Nothing happened. It was locked, of course. I should have thought that a door to a tower used as a prison would be kept locked.

CHAPTER 46

Maybe it was just stiff. I twisted the ring again even harder and yanked the door with all my strength. I rested one foot on the ground and put the other one on the wall of the tower so that I could pull using all my body weight. I gave an almighty heave.

Still nothing.

I twisted the ring the other way and tried again. Maybe locks in Dralfynia worked the opposite way to back home. Sweat popped out on my forehead, and my arms and fingers hurt from the strain of twisting and pulling at the same time.

I grimaced with the effort and, bracing myself, I gave one last huge tug. My fingers were damp with sweat and slipped from the metal ring. I was still struggling to cope with the glass slippers and having to balance on heels. I fell over and landed flat on my back. I lay there panting for a second, tempted to give up, then I remembered the sound of Olive's voice. I struggled to my feet and gave the door an annoyed kick.

It gently swung open an inch.

It wasn't magic; it wasn't even locked. The door just opened inwards, and I had been pulling it outwards.

My face burned red with shame. I was very, very grateful that I was invisible and no one had seen me make such a fool of myself.

Relieved, I slipped through the door and gently pushed it shut behind me. I looked around. I was in a roughly circular room. There was nothing there except for a stone staircase that spiraled up into the darkness above me. I started to climb it. It was very narrow and each step was hardly wide enough to fit my foot. On my right was the tower wall and on my left was a drop to the floor below. The higher I climbed, the longer, darker and more frightening that drop grew. I kept one hand on the stone wall as I climbed. I hoped that if I started to fall, I would be able to save myself by clawing wildly with my fingernails. There were no torches on the walls, or any other kind of lighting, so I had to feel each step with my toes to make sure it was safe to transfer my weight.

Round and round and up and up I went. Occasionally I passed narrow windows cut into the stone wall. They let in a faint grayness from outside which was a relief because then I could see a step or two ahead of me. I peeped through each one and saw only the land at the rear of the castle. There, far below me, were the middens, or rubbish heaps, where we had hidden on our last visit to Timaru. I gave a little shudder as I remembered the living carpet of rats we had seen. There were people moving around—they looked so small I could hardly tell if they were human. I guessed they were some of the castle's servants by the drab colors they wore, although I saw a flash of greeny-gold as one wealthy person walked along. I hoped it wasn't the prince. I really wanted him to be in his chambers getting to know Edith and Agatha.

The more I climbed in the glass slippers, the more my feet began to hurt. Already painful where the cartwheel had rolled over me, now the sharp edges of the glass were rubbing against my heels and I knew that I had big blisters developing. There were no thick soles to cushion my feet either, like modern shoes have, so the bottoms of my feet began to ache. I stopped, wondering whether to take them off altogether, but I didn't know if there were more guards at the top of the tower so I struggled on. I decided that even when I grew up, I would never, ever wear high-heeled shoes.

Finally, I could see light coming from above. I rounded the last bend and found myself rising into the middle of a large, round chamber with one wide, barred window.

There was a table and a bench, a narrow wooden bed, a wood-en-framed mirror with a cloth thrown over most of it, and even a pretty mat on the floor. It all looked quite comfortable. Sitting at the table was a girl. She looked a few years older than me and she was dressed in very flattering rags. She was sewing a medium-sized patch onto a large patch. Nearby was a small patch, ready to be sewn onto the medium-sized one. She was incredibly pretty. I felt a little jealous stab as I remembered that she and Aidan were friends. Then another thought occurred to me. I frowned. If I had just climbed up to the chamber so easily, why didn't Ellie just go down the stairs and out of the tower? That door wasn't guarded.

Why hadn't she just walked out?

CHAPTER 47

I didn't want to frighten Ellie by suddenly becoming visible again after taking my shoes off, so I spoke first. "Ahem, I don't mean to frighten you," I said.

She screamed anyway. I think a voice coming from thin air might have been more terrifying than a twelve-year-old girl suddenly appearing, even if she was dressed as Prince Charming.

"Shush," I whispered, frantically clicking the bows and pulling the glass slippers off. "I'm a friend of Aidan's. I'm here to rescue you," I told her. Then I sat down and started to massage my feet. Oh, it was wonderful. I stretched my toes apart and enjoyed how it felt for my feet to feel free again.

"Really?" she said. There was doubt in her voice. "Aren't you just a …" I looked at her with narrowed eyes. Yes, I was a kid, but there was no "just a" about me or any of my friends. I wiggled my toes. It felt like bliss.

"Ahhhh," I said.

"Ah ha!" said a tiny, squeaky voice. I looked around me in surprise. I had thought that Ellie and I were alone in the tower room. I had been looking forward to a nice chat so I could explain who I was and how great and brave I was to come right into the Beast's castle to save her. Now it seemed that there was someone else here.

"I've caught you," said the voice.

"You've caught me?" I said. I needed to check because I still didn't see anyone, and I definitely didn't feel like I had been captured. And after our earlier trip to Dralfynia, I certainly knew what it felt like to be captured.

"Look down," said Ellie. I did. There stood a little mouse with a big attitude. She wore a purple velvet jacket and had her front paws on her hips. She had bright black eyes, white whiskers and was very familiar.

"The prince and I knew that her friends would come to get her. I saw her rescue some of your fellow traitors and I told the prince someone would be sure to come for her. You've fallen into my cunning trap."

I recognized this tiny, furry villain. It was Mrs. Mouse. Last time we were here, Olive had persuaded her to help rescue us when we were held prisoner in the castle dungeon. It seemed that she wasn't going to be so helpful this time, and she obviously thought she had trapped us. Except that she was just a mouse and we were two girls. We could still just walk out.

"Look, I'll explain everything later," I said to Ellie, ignoring Mrs. Mouse. I was puzzled that she was still sitting down. "We'll just get on our way then," I hinted.

"Hey, are those my shoes?" she said suddenly, pointing at the glass slippers. I pushed out my bottom lip while I thought about it. I supposed that she was right, according to the fairy tale anyway, but they had to go to the Island of Merthyr so she couldn't keep them. And was the middle of my daring rescue really the time to be talking about shoes? I pulled my sneakers from my pocket and slipped my feet into them.

Boy, that really did feel good.

Ellie came over to me and picked up the glass slippers before I could stop her. As she was stooped over them, she whispered to me from the side of her mouth. It was difficult to understand what she said, but I heard enough to realize that I wasn't going to be rescuing anyone; I was in trouble. Again. She was letting me know that I had walked straight into a trap.

"You shouldn't have come here," she hissed. "It's a full moon this week and that darned mouse is already up on the window ledge, ready to call the guard."

A guard that was outside the tower? I laughed. There was no way we'd be caught unless it could fly. Wait a minute. Had she said full moon? Then I remembered seeing a flash of greeny-gold outside.

That probably meant the real guard was a certain were-dragon who I had already really annoyed, who'd be pretty pleased to have both the glass slippers for her collection and who was strolling between the rubbish pits right now, just a short flight away. The cunning Mrs. Mouse was already scampering down the tower wall to get her.

No wonder it had been so easy to get into the tower.

I could only think of one thing to do.

"Let's run," I said. I jumped to my feet, grabbing the glass slippers and shoving them back into my bag. I seized hold of Ellie's arm and started to drag her with me to the staircase.

The room went dark.

Something was outside the window, blocking the light from the fading sun.

CHAPTER
48

"Ellie!"

"Aidan!" Ellie pulled herself free and ran to the window, the opposite direction I wanted her to go in. In fact, she was climbing up onto the window ledge and smiling. I looked past her and saw Aidan's head and Rory's head bobbing in mid-air.

I ran over to join Ellie, and realized that they were sitting on Ruggy and floating level with the window. They pointed down, and I saw Mrs. Mouse had already almost reached the base of the tower.

"Quick," I called, shoving Ellie further out of the window. "Latrina Earwax is down there and that mouse is the one who told the Beast that Ellie rescued us. She's going to get the were-dragon."

Rory and Aidan twisted their necks to look down. Then they unexpectedly started to scramble forward across Ruggy in our direction. Aidan leaped the few inches between Ruggy and the window ledge and burst through the window, knocking Ellie and me onto our backs on the floor.

"Too late," he gasped. "She's coming." I stood up and looked out of the window. Rory, the cuddly little ginger bear cub, sat on Ruggy, terrified. His short legs couldn't have managed the leap. He was shaking from snout to tail, and his huge brown eyes were bright with tears of fright. I could see why. A genuine, honest-to-goodness dragon was speeding up the tower from the ground. It was big and fast. It had scales that shimmered gold and green, and puffs of white smoke came in a plume from each nostril, which was cute on Clyde, but terrifying on a dragon. It had a face I recognized. Latrina Earwax stared up at me; in a few moments, we would be eyeball to eyeball.

Rory whimpered.

"Ruggy!" I screamed. "Get out of here; get away!" And then, a miracle. The most uncooperative flying carpet in the world did what he was told. He gave a lurch, and Rory was being flown higher and away to safety.

He might be safe for now, but we weren't. The were-dragon was like an elephant rampaging through the jungle. She head-butted the window. Although there was no glass in the window, there were metal bars, which I guessed were there to stop people falling out—and dragons getting in. She smashed into the bars, bending them with the force of the impact.

The three of us hurriedly backed away. She flew off and I breathed again. Perhaps we could still escape. But she had been circling so that she could return seconds later, flying harder and faster. Bam! She smashed into the bars again. This time, the central bar snapped completely, falling to the ground in the room with a clang. I reached out and grabbed it. It would be a good weapon.

"We need to get out of here," I said. We turned to the top of the spiral staircase and felt another jarring smash. The whole of the top of the tower shuddered. I risked a glance back. The were-dragon had forced her head through the shattered remains of the metal bars. She glared at me hungrily.

Eek.

Then her cheeks puffed out and a stream of flames flew from her nostrils. She wasn't far enough into the room for the fire to reach us, but we felt a searing heat on our skin.

"Meera," Ellie yelled. She ran across the room and grabbed the mirror I had noticed when I arrived. Clutching it under her arm, she ran back. I half pushed her down the stairs.

"Get going," I told her. "If we get separated, don't wait. Look for a really huge unicorn and you'll be OK." Aidan tried to wait for me, but I shoved him after Ellie.

"Run," I said to him. "I'm right behind you." But I wasn't. As I took my turn to start down the narrow stairs, Latrina Earwax had wheeled through the sky one more time and battered into the building again. I fell to my knees with the impact, unable to keep my footing. The tower was hit again and, as I sprawled forward on my stomach, I felt something grab my ankle.

CHAPTER
49

I screamed out in fear and pain as claws sank into my flesh and I felt myself being pulled backward. I scrabbled to grab hold of the stone flags that made up the floor, but they had been worn smooth over the years. My fingernails just scraped painfully across the surface, splintering but doing nothing to slow me down—I was still being dragged back toward Latrina.

I could feel a terrific heat coming from the mouth of the were-dragon and the tiny hairs on my leg started to curl. I twisted away as best as I could and managed to roll over from my stomach to my back. I let my gaze travel down my body to my leg and onward to my foot. I saw the vicious talons slicing into my ankle. I looked higher up and straight into the dull, hateful eyes of Latrina Earwax. She opened her mouth wide and I saw a row of jagged, sharp teeth—then I spotted a second row behind them. They curved inward. If she bit something, there would be no chance of it pulling itself free—and she was going to bite me.

I tightened my grip on the metal bar that had fallen from the window and I aimed it at her neck. I had a strong arm and good accuracy after years of playing softball. I pitched with all my might and the bar flew from my hand. It pierced her scales, sending out a trickle of green blood. Yes! I had her!

She turned her head and glanced down at the bar. She pulled back her lips and, baring those awful teeth, she nipped at the bar. Then she jerked it out with her mouth, spitting it to the ground as if it was nothing more than a tooth pick.

Although I was so panicked that I could hardly breathe or think clearly, I instinctively lashed out with my free foot, kicking frantically at anything I could find. My first attempt landed on the talons that were dragging me to her and did no damage. I wished I still had on the glass slipper, at least it had heels and would have cut her. That gave me an idea. I twisted my foot and lashed out again. The silver buckle on my sneakers might cause a little damage. It worked better than I could have dreamed. It sliced through her tough scales as if they were cream cheese and a fountain of the green blood spurted out from the small cut. I yanked my leg back, almost ripping my buckle loose.

Latrina gave a deafening roar of pain and anger and reared back, holding up her wounded limb. The blood was gushing everywhere and all her attention was on her injury. I snatched my opportunity, scrambled to the top of the winding stairs and began to run down them.

My feet already hurt from the glass slippers and the damage from the cartwheel, but my bruised ankle was far worse as it throbbed and burned from the were-dragon's claw marks. I had been so careful when I crept up the narrow stairs but now, despite the long drop into darkness, I had to risk falling to get away. I was sobbing with fear and pain and I raced as fast as I could, hugging the side wall and tripping over the silver buckle that now flapped around as I went.

From above me, I could hear bellows that sounded full of rage, hate and agony. There were violent crashes. I could only imagine what was happening but I figured that the were-dragon was smashing as much of the tower as she could to try and get at us.

I increased my speed, guessing that I would only have a few seconds before she worked out that she couldn't fit down the staircase and changed the focus of her attack to the courtyard below which was where we would all be heading next. But I couldn't maintain my speed and keep my footing. There was a terrific smash from above me and the entire tower vibrated wildly. I waved my arms to keep my balance and grabbed at the wall but I stood on the loose buckle with my other foot and began to fall down into the darkness. I didn't know how far I had to fall and had just opened my mouth to scream when I hit something with a "whumpff". It was something soft. It was something that had a bear cub on it. It was Ruggy, once again saving one of us.

"We have to get out of here," I gasped at Rory. I was shaking with fear as dust and chunks of stone started to drift down on us from the damage being wreaked above.

"No chance," he answered. "The courtyard's full of guards. As soon as the were-dragon started to attack, they came running from all over to see what was going on. We rushed in here to hide." He floated us down to the entrance to the tower. I saw Aidan, Olive and Ellie waiting for us.

"Where's Persis?" I demanded. I hopped off of Ruggy, wincing as I did. "And where's Clyde? Are they both out there?" The others looked at each other.

"Clyde couldn't fit in the doorway," said Olive in a small voice. I felt my stomach drop.

"Persis?" No one answered. "Don't tell me she's been captured again," I said, hardly daring to believe it. The last time we were in Dralfynia, she was the first to be captured by the goblins, then she was captured along with the rest of us by the guards.

"Not exactly, no," said Olive. "She's fast asleep."

CHAPTER 50

"We heard he was looking for a bride to make his princess, and that's going to be one of us," said Enid firmly. They towered menacingly over the guards who were trying to stop them from entering the Beast's chambers in the castle. A barred door had, for the time being, stopped the tidal wave that was Enid and Agatha. The guards they had dragged along clambered to their feet and cowered under the Sisters' forceful glares. One guard was slightly braver than the others.

"You can't go in; he's practicing his card tricks. And actually, he only wants to meet real princesses, which you're not" he told them. The other guards took a step away from him and looked around everywhere but at him.

"What! Are you saying that an ordinary Dralfynian woman ain't good enough for him and he wants to take a bride from another country?" roared Enid, her eyes crossing in her anger.

"Uh, um, yes, that's right," squeaked the guard. "You know, for political reasons." He took a step toward the other guards, but they quickly pushed him back.

"Hang on," said Agatha. She looked crafty. She nudged Enid with her shoulder, hard enough to make anyone else go flying. Enid scowled at her. Agatha tossed her head in the direction of Clyde, Persis, Aidan and Olive. A few seconds later, Enid gave a slow nod.

"It just so happens," the Sisters said in unison, "that we have a 'real' princess with us. But," added Agatha, holding up a warning hand, "she ain't allowed to go nowhere without us. We're her stylists, see? Sleeping Beauty over there wants to investigate his spinning wheel, but we have to go with her. Understand?" The poor guard nodded miserably to indicate 'Yes, he understood', but Enid and Agatha chose to misinterpret this as 'Yes, you can go in'.

"And," said Enid, "she wants to wait in the corridor or somewhere else while we see the prince first, OK?" By this time, the guard had given up. He stepped aside and scuttled over to the other guards who were carefully watching a very interesting fly buzzing around a heap of straw.

"You're going to be in big trouble for letting them in," one of the others told him. He looked back at the Sisters who were now dragging Persis from Clyde's back.

"Not as much trouble as the prince," he said.

"But I'm not the real Sleeping Beauty," Persis argued, kicking and wriggling for all she was worth. She had been slung over Enid's shoulder and found that she was talking to her back.

"Don't be silly," Agatha told her as they strode through the now unguarded door and into the depths of the castle. "You're always yawning and you got that floaty dress on. 'Course you're her. They got a very special spinning wheel, just for you."

Persis had a very strange view of her journey into the castle. Everything she saw was going backward and being bounced up and down, and she only saw things that were a foot from the ground. She worked out they were traveling along a passageway and caught glimpses of the bottoms of doors, woven mats and the legs of pieces of furniture.

"How do you know where to go?" she asked, as she was carried in a route that zig-zagged up and down, left and right.

"Oh don't worry about that. We can sniff out an unmarried prince from a mile away," Enid told her.

"And an unmarried duke or lord from half a mile," added Agatha. Enid dumped Persis to the ground in a small room. It was obviously a waiting room because almost one whole wall was taken up by grand doors that must have led into a great chamber. The Sisters immediately turned their backs on her and began to check out their appearances in a mirror.

"Ooooo, you look lovely," Enid cooed as she huffed into her cupped hand and then sniffed to see if her breath was smelly.

"Thanks, dear. You look lovely too," said Agatha, polishing her only tooth with her fingertip. "One of us is bound to be chosen this time."

"That's right. You know what they say? Forty-seventh time's a charm," said Enid. And with that, they flung open the double doors and strode through them, leaving them to slam in their wake—and leaving a completely confused Persis behind them.

"What just happened?" she said aloud. "I need to get out of here." She looked around to find her way back to the courtyard. The passage she had been brought along was to her right, so she turned to walk down it, figuring that if she got lost, she would just ask someone for directions. As she stepped into the passage, she felt something tugging her by the arm, back the way she had just come. She looked around, but saw nothing. She took another step, then another. OK, now she was moving. Then there was a definite yank on her arm. She whirled around and stared. Was this Sabrina in her invisible shoes playing a joke again?

"Stop fooling around, Brina," she said, uncertainly. She started to walk backward, away from the little room she had been left in. Her left arm stayed where she put it, by her side, but her right arm was pulled upward.

Except, she realized, nothing was pulling her or holding her arm. It was acting all by itself. It floated up and in front of her, and then it suddenly pulled her forward: she couldn't control her own arm.

"This place is getting too weird for words," she grumbled. She took hold of the contrary right arm with her left hand and pulled it into her body again, then started to walk to the passageway. To her great surprise, her right arm pulled itself free and smacked her left arm. She stared down at her hands and then found herself tugged hard toward a shadowy corner of the room. She looked over to see what she was being hauled toward. It was a wooden seat, and next to it was a wooden wheel that had wooden arms and levers—and a long, very pointy needle, which gleamed with a green light. It was the spindle on a spinning wheel. The kind that could send her to sleep for a hundred years, if the fairy tale was right.

She clenched her knees to keep from moving, but the power of the spindle calling to her hand was too strong. She was dragged along, leaving two gouges in the wooden floors where her heels had dug in. She was powerless to stop her finger as it reached for the glowing needle.

CHAPTER 51

"**W**hen Agatha and Enid got thrown out of the prince's chamber, they came back and told us what had happened. They didn't get the chance to rescue Persis because the prince was talking about introducing them to his pet dragon, so they were running. They said something about seeing why people called him the Beast and added that they had moved on now. They were heading off to visit a lord in a neighboring kingdom whose wife had just died. Then all the guards came out to see what the were-dragon was doing, the Sisters ran off, and we ran in here," Aidan explained.

OK, we were trapped in the bottom of a tower which was being attacked by a were-dragon. Our only other way out was through a door that had the Beast's guards on the other side of it, waiting to pounce on whoever came out. Clyde was surrounded by soldiers and Persis was twenty minutes into her hundred-year sleep somewhere inside the castle.

To top it all off, Olive was suddenly sick. She went to the side of the room and threw up. Rory scratched at his hind quarters, sending a cloud of ginger bear fur into the air. I looked at him. His fur was starting to look patchy. I wondered if he was molting. I ignored Olive, though. She pukes a lot.

We obviously needed a plan. I knew our plans were usually terrible, but this time, we also needed more than a plan. We needed some blind luck.

Then, as a complete surprise to us all, blind luck was just what we got.

The entire tower gave a huge shudder as somewhere overhead Latrina flung her body again into the shattered remains of the top room. A torrent of dust and chunks of stone poured down on us and there was a tearing sound as if stone walls were being wrenched apart, grating and groaning as they went. The noise sent our hands to our ears to block it out. If we didn't risk the guards, we would be crushed under tons of rock.

"Psst," said our blind luck. Our hands over our ears meant we didn't hear the sound, but we felt a sudden gust of air from behind us. We turned to see what had happened. Had the back of the tower fallen already? Instead, we saw that a section of the curved wall had cracked apart neatly and slid backward, making a door. In the crack we saw two eyes looking at us. We dropped our hands and this time we heard "Psstt!"

Then we saw a hand beckoning us to go into the crack in the wall. Since we were out of options we hurried over and, one by one, squeezed through the narrow gap. I went first. I turned sideways and forced my shoulder through. The rough stone scraped my cheek and I had a frightening moment when I thought I was stuck, but then I was on the other side. After me came Rory. He pushed Ruggy through first and I grabbed him, then held Rory's paw as he squeezed through. His little tummy was all squashed, but he made it. Then came Olive and Ellie, who both slid through elegantly. Aidan stood on the other side, hesitating. His muscles from working at the inn made him broader than us. He wasn't sure he would fit through, and neither were we.

"Hurry up," said a woman. "I'll pull the door as much as I can if you take his arm and haul him through." She gripped the section of stone wall that had moved and braced herself to pull. It shifted a tiny amount more.

Aidan launched himself sideways into the gap and Olive and I took hold of his shoulder and arm.

"On the count of three, pull," instructed the woman.

"One," she began. Then there was another massive judder and the tower began to shake. We screamed and pulled. Aidan yelled and pushed. The woman cried out and yanked at the door, and finally he was through, pushing Olive and me to the ground as he landed on us. We were so relieved we started to laugh.

"This is no time for playing, you young foals," said the woman sternly. She put her back to the door and pushed, forcing it closed as much as she could. She looked at the door. There was still a crack showing. She shook her head.

"It'll have to do," she said. She turned on her heel and started to walk quickly away from us. We looked at each other, shrugged and followed her. We were in a very narrow passage that seemed to run through a gap between the walls of different rooms. She set a fast pace and with my injured leg I struggled to keep up with her. I went to tuck the loose buckle into my sock so that I wouldn't trip as I ran, but it had become firmly sewn into place again. I remembered again that whatever we wore in Dralfynia, we were stuck with until we got back to Melas again.

"Is this a secret passageway?" asked Rory.

"Of course it is," said the woman with surprise in her voice. "All castles have secret passageways."

She stopped suddenly. I bumped into her. Rory bumped into me. Olive bumped into Rory, and Aidan—well, you get the picture. The woman ran her hands over the wall.

"Three stones left and two up," she said. Then she pushed hard and a section of the wall opened silently. This door was obviously in better condition than the one in the tower. She led the way and soon we were all standing in a room filled with bookshelves, globes on stands, and tables covered in maps and crystals. There were comfortable chairs and the walls were decorated with paintings. An empty picture stand stood in an alcove.

"Hey," said Olive. "I've been here before." I saw that she recognized the table covered with parchment and the feathers to write with.

"Finally I'm back!" said a sulky voice, making us all jump. "Just be a sweetie, Ellie, and pop me back on my stand, would you?"

CHAPTER 52

Ellie had carried the mirror that she had grabbed from the tower all the way through our escape, although she had dropped the cloth somewhere along the way. Now she placed it carefully on the stand in the alcove. In its dusty glass I could see a face. The eyes darted around the room, taking everything in.

"A bit of a polish would be nice, thanks very much," it grumbled. Ellie pulled one of the many patches from her dress and rubbed at the mirror.

"Hey, that tickles," it giggled.

"Sorry, Meera," she said, giving it a final swipe. "There, good as new." The mirror frowned when its eyes rested on Olive.

"What," it said, in a voice full of horror, "have you done to your hair, girl?" Olive's hand touched the loop-de-loop braids. Her lower lip trembled. "And who are the rest of you?" it added, looking each one of us up and down as if we were revolting specimens.

"I was just about to ask the same question," said the woman who had led us to the room. She walked slowly up and down in front of us, while inspecting us thoroughly. I took the opportunity to inspect her right

Michele Clark McConnochie | 165

back. She wore riding clothes. Dirty, knee-length boots, a smart jacket covered in brown smears, and grubby jodhpurs. She had very messy gray hair piled on top of her head and held in place by dozens of bobby pins. She smelled like Clyde.

"Your Grace," said Ellie, "this is my friend Aidan." She pointed at him and he nodded his head respectfully. "And these are … well, I don't know who these people are," she admitted. I opened my mouth to explain who we were, then shut it again.

Who were we? Sabrina and Rory Summers, and Olive Ayres? Or Prince Charming, Baby Bear and Goldilocks? I looked at Aidan, hoping he would help me out, but he was too busy having his arm shaken up and down like a water-pump handle. His head wobbled a little from the vigorousness of the woman's handshake.

"Aidan, pleased to meet you," she exclaimed. "You're from my home-town of Tylwyth Teg, aren't you? Jill's lad—from the Inn of the Fluffy Kitten? How's the family?" Her voice boomed around the room. I knew that we still had to deal with a were-dragon, guards and a Beast and wondered if this was the time for socializing.

"They're fine, thank you, Your Grace," he said. "These are some visitors. We're all very grateful that you rescued us." This must be Duchess Yvonne, I thought. The one who was standing in for the missing Princess Heidi until it was time for her, or any children she might have had—or for the Beast—to take over ruling Dralfynia.

I had imagined someone much more regal than the woman who was staring at us. No, not at us. At me. She walked over to me and bent her face close to mine. She stared hard for a long time. Her eyes narrowed.

"What's your name, my dear, and where are you from?" she said. I felt as if I was on a TV game show. "And I have met the real Prince Charming many times, by the way," she said suddenly. There was a glint in her eye that seemed to be saying "Better tell the truth this time, Sabrina; I can see right through you, you know."

"Sabrina," I managed to say. "Sabrina Summers. I live in Melas." She looked puzzled. "It's a very distant land," I explained. I assumed that it was, but I didn't really know if it was distant in terms of miles, time, or space—or whatever. I pointed at Rory. "This is my little brother, Rory," I said. The duchess shook her head.

"Your mother married twice, I presume?" she asked. Even for Dralfynia, having a brother who was not human must have been strange. Then she noticed that Rory was holding Ruggy and her eyes widened. She turned back to me again and looked at my bag. The outline of the glass slippers was clearly visible under the cloth. Her eyes widened even more.

If this had been a cartoon instead of real life, a lightbulb would have appeared above her head. It was obvious that she recognized the magic objects.

The mirror interrupted.

"Vonnie, I hate to interrupt your little chat, but really, time is of the essence," it said dramatically. "You know how I hate to be rushed and I just know you're going to be asking for my help, yet again. And what do I even get out of it? The occasional flick-over with a dirty cloth. Hardly even a thank you. Nobody really understands what it's like to be a magic mirror these days. And another thing …" and on and on Meera went, complaining and griping until Duchess Yvonne brought her hand down hard on one of the tables.

"Be quiet, Meera," she said. "You were right in pointing out that time is short. The prince blames me for anything that goes wrong, so he'll be here in two shakes of a thoroughbred's tail. We need to work out an escape to plan for these people."

"And a rescue," I said. We still had to find Persis.

CHAPTER 53

When Olive explained to Duchess Yvonne that Persis had pricked her finger on a spinning wheel outside the Beast's chamber, she had clapped her hand to her mouth and reeled back a couple of steps.

I think that meant things were bad. Then Meera joined in. "Not the poisoned spinning wheel," it gasped. "It's a total disaster. There's nothing to be done. Completely pointless. Might as well all give up now. Hopeless, hopeless, hopeless."

This was the most immature and irritating magic mirror I had ever met.

"What's the problem?" I asked.

"I think Meera was dropped when she was a youngster," said the duchess, looking over at the mirror.

"No, I meant, what's the problem with Persis?"

"Oh. She'll have to sleep for a hundred years because the poison in that particular spindle, or needle, acts as a sleeping spell."

"But we need to get back," I protested. My dad would be worrying about me because we would be late home from detention, but I was also starting to worry about Olive and Rory's health. Olive was looking pale and kept putting her fingers to her mouth as if she felt sick, and Rory was starting to shed fur quite heavily now. If they were unwell, they would need a doctor—or maybe a veterinarian.

"Back, my dear?" The duchess looked at me firmly. "Back to where, exactly. And just why do you have my family's magic objects?"

They were great questions. I just wish I had a great answer. I looked over at Olive, hoping she would understand my warning. Olive had a habit of telling grown-ups the truth and trusting them, but she didn't say a word. I figured she wasn't sure about the Duchess Yvonne yet either. Personally, I had two doubts about her.

One: if there was a secret passage and she knew Ellie was being held prisoner in the tower, why had she waited for a were-dragon attack before rescuing her?

Two: why hadn't she taken over running Dralfynia properly instead of just looking after it while the Beast went around setting up armies and looking for magic objects?

"Your Grace," said Aidan. Oh no, not another honest friend. "Sabrina, Olive, Rory and their friend Persis are visitors from another kingdom as they said, but they are sworn enemies of the Beast with Eight Fingers and are helping us. It is our mission to take the glass slippers and the flying carpet to the Island of Merthyr, where your sister and brother-in-law will keep them until the rightful heir is found."

At the mention of the retired king and queen, the duchess gave a big horse-like snort.

"We wouldn't be in this pickle if they hadn't retired so early and gone off to the Island of Merthyr," she said. "And that son of theirs needed some discipline when he was young. Hazel was always too soft on him if you ask me. Now I'm dumped with all this pointless work when I'm far too busy to bother with it." I guess that answered my second question.

I guess sisters and brothers still squabble, even when they are grown up. She suddenly swung around to Rory, who was biting a chunk of fur from one of his legs. I saw that the skin below was sore and red. I looked over at Olive. She was now sitting down with her head between her knees, breathing deeply.

"Boy?" said the duchess.

"Yeah?" said Rory. I saw her eyes flash in annoyance.

"It's 'Yes Your Grace'," she corrected him. But she had the sense to carry on speaking before he could point out that it was just as rude to call him "boy". "Tell me, have you seen these objects being used?"

"Yessssssssssssssssssssss, Your Grace," said Rory sarcastically. "Brina and I have flown Ruggy and she's worn the glass slippers and gone invisible."

"Ruggy? Oh, you mean the Royal Flying Carpet. And those," she added, pointing to my bag, "are the Royal Glass Slippers." She was silent as she thought about what Rory had told her. Then she nodded slowly several times. There were a few more lightbulbs going on.

"Excellent news," she said. "We will need you both to make this escape work."

CHAPTER 54

Meera was playing hard to get. She pouted and sulked, and it wasn't until Ellie threatened to clean her with vinegar that she finally tuned in to show us where Persis was sleeping. We all crowded around and looked at the cloudy image.

"Wow, she looks so pretty," said Rory, surprised. He was right, though. She had lain down on a bench next to the spinning wheel. It was covered in cushions and blankets. Her hair was spread out like it does when you dip the back of your head underwater in the bathtub and her face was calm and smiling slightly.

"She looks so happy, too," I said. "It's going to be a shame to wake her up. By the way, how do we do that, exactly?"

"Haven't you been listening?" snapped Meera. "You have to wait a hundred years."

"No, I mean, how do we really wake her up?" I insisted. Dad had read me enough bedtime stories when I was little for me to know there was always a way out.

"True love's kiss?" suggested Olive, hesitantly.

"Eeoowww," Rory and I said in unison. Yuk. That sounded gross. We each pulled a face.

"Don't be so silly, girl," said Duchess Yvonne. "You need the antidote to the spell on the spindle, that's all."

"Oh good, and what's that exactly?" I asked.

"The sleeping spell is so powerful because it has been cast by Witchy Wu Ling." I thought I knew the one she meant but the last time that it had been used on Persis, she'd woken up only a few minutes later and we hadn't needed any antidote stuff. "The Beast had her develop a really powerful version to use as a weapon. This was a test batch and he's been waiting for some silly girl to come along and try it. I'm afraid that if you want your friend to wake up in the next hundred years, you will have to give her the antidote," said the duchess. "That's a potion that will cure the poison."

"Pah!" shrieked Meera. "Good luck with that," she sneered. "It's in Witchy Wu's cottage and she's got the bakers in doing her rebuild. It'll be a nightmare finding it!"

I was getting fed up with the duchess and Meera. We were so close to getting everything done that we had to and all I wanted was to get to the Island of Merthyr, leave Ruggy and the glass slippers there and go home. Grumpily, I demanded that the duchess tell me how we were going to escape and mentally added a detour to Scary Forest to the rest of our journey: woo hoo.

As she opened her mouth to speak, we felt the building shudder and heard screaming and yelling from below. We rushed to the window and peered out into the night. What we saw made our blood do the cold and runny thing all over again. Silhouetted against the dark sky was the shape of a dragon. From its nostrils came sparks and plumes of smoke.

We had arrived in Timaru in the morning, we had wasted hours of our precious time on getting involved with the Sisters, rescuing Ellie and the dragon attack—and now evening was falling.

"She's still attacking the tower," I said.

"She's going to have quite a headache in the morning," said Meera.

"How can she be a were-dragon in daylight?" Olive wanted to know. "I'd have thought they could only come out when the moon was up."

"No, they are active for one week a month. They are strongest when the moon is up. You have seen her at her weakest. But I think she's stopped for now. She's running out of flames at last," said Duchess Yvonne, pointing upward. "She'll have to go and change back to a human being for a while to recharge. That's good," she said, shooing us away from the windows. "We can get you all away now. We'll need help, of course. There are far too many of you to go on the flying carpet." I did a quick headcount. Once we had Persis with us that would make six.

"My friends the White Widows will help," explained the duchess. "We'll send some of you on the carpet, the others can go with them and you should all be with my sister well before daybreak." I remembered Clyde, but Aidan beat me to it.

"We have our unicorn with us, too," he said. For the first time, I saw the duchess get excited.

"Is that your Clydesdale in the courtyard?" We nodded. "A fine beast, very impressive. Must be eighteen hands I'd say. Puts my little fallabellas to shame I must say, ha ha." I had no idea what she was talking about. Hands? I thought horses had hooves. And what on earth were fallabellas? Some kind of a little bell maybe? I learned later they were super cute little horses.

Quickly Duchess Yvonne outlined her plan. She would send Clyde ahead on foot (or do I mean on hoof?) to meet us in Scary Forest. Then she arranged for Aidan, Ellie and me to go and find Persis. She decided that a bear wandering through Timaru Castle would attract attention, so Rory would stay behind with Olive to help him. He was needed to pilot Ruggy again.

"In the dark?" he asked, his voice very small.

"Yes, lad, but don't worry. There are as many terrifying things out to get you in daylight as in the dark you know." I don't think she cheered him up.

I ignored my blisters and forced my swollen feet into the glass slippers again. The plan was for me to go ahead and let Aidan and Ellie know if it was safe for them to follow me, but Ellie would guide me in the right direction.

"Ellie will have to seek haven on the Island of Merthyr," said Yvonne. "It's not safe for her here. That ridiculous mouse who betrayed her has friends everywhere and if they see Ellie, they will let my nephew know and he'll come after me too." For a moment, she looked genuinely scared and that answered my first question.

Oh well, the more the merrier, I thought. One more person who was from Dralfynia might be helpful. I grimaced as I stood up—I had forgotten how sore my injured ankle and both my poor feet were. I tried to think about other things to keep my mind from the pain. Things like how close it was to dawn on our third day in Dralfynia, how terrifying it would be to go to the gingerbread cottage again, and how great it would be to have sticking plasters covering my blisters.

CHAPTER 55

We set off. I limped ahead, following Ellie's whispered instructions. The castle seemed quiet. When we had looked out of the window in the duchess' rooms we saw that most of the guards were busy having to put out several small fires caused by Latrina Earwax. It meant that we were able to find our way to the chamber where Persis had fallen asleep without being challenged.

I hadn't really needed Ellie's directions. In fact, the nearer we got, the more difficult it was to hear her whispering anyway. Persis' snoring was like having three dentists' drills in your mouth at the same time. I felt the ground beneath my feet vibrating. She broke up the drilling by adding in a few snorts and snuffles. She had looked so pretty but she sounded just terrible!

One more corridor and we were there. We stood and looked down at her. We needed to get her to the window so that we could push her out of it and onto Ruggy. I gave her shoulder a shake. It made no difference. I bent down and hissed into her ear, "Persis, you need to move." That made no difference either. "Persis, if you don't get up right now, I'm going to tear up your signed US Women's National Soccer Team poster." Still nothing. That's when I knew for sure that she was well and truly enchanted. I grabbed both of her shoulders, one with each hand, and shook her hard. She yawned, stretched, turned over and settled back down. She was so relaxed that she was even dribbling a little bit.

Sheesh.

"We'll have to carry her," I said. I took her feet and Aidan and Ellie grabbed her under the armpits. I knew that if she was at all awake, she'd be shrieking and wriggling. She really hates being tickled under the armpits. It's my secret weapon against her when we're play-fighting.

We lifted her on the count of three and immediately dropped her onto the floor with a huge booming bang. I heard movement from behind a huge door that led from the little room we were in. There were heavy footsteps from behind it. Someone was coming.

"Quickly," I said, fighting down panic. We tried again. She was heavy and long and floppy. We managed to drag her across the floor and over to a window, then Ellie and Aidan propped her upright so that the wall was supporting her.

The handle of the door to the other room twisted.

Persis gave a happy snuffle and slid down the wall until she was sitting upright.

Why was nothing in my life simple? I told Aidan and Ellie to climb onto the window ledge. They crouched there and held out their arms. I pulled one of Persis' limp arms up and handed it to Aidan, then I did the same with the other arm, handing it to Ellie.

"Pull," I told them.

The door to the other room opened a crack.

Aidan and Ellie gave a huge yank and Persis began to rise until she looked as if she was standing with her arms above her head. I crouched down and wrapped my arms around her legs. Using my shoulder to act as a seat for her, I pushed myself upward, forcing my muscles to work harder than they knew how. Grunting, I gave a huge thrust and then Persis was sitting on the window ledge, supported by Aidan and Ellie.

The door banged open.

In the doorway stood a huge figure, a man who was tall and broad. He was wearing a woollen cloak with the hood pulled up, hiding his face. It was held together by a gold toggle.

"How dare you enter my castle without my permission," he roared. He shook his left hand at us. It was a hand with one thumb and two fingers on it. The Beast with Eight Fingers started to stride across to the window. I hoped Ruggy was waiting outside. I gave Persis' feet a final shove and sent the three of them toppling out of the window into the smoky night air. The Beast gave a bellow and ran toward me. Even though I was invisible, I was still terrified of being caught. I turned my back on him and placed my hands flat on the ledge and then I hauled myself up so that I was crouched and ready to jump out of the window onto Ruggy.

He swiped at where I knelt as he reached past me for the others but his hand connected with my injured ankle. I gave a yelp of pain.

It took him all of three seconds to understand that if there was someone invisible in his castle, they had stolen one glass slipper from Latrina Earwax and found the other. And now they were here in his castle, wearing two of the objects he needed to help him become king.

He gave a thunderous yell and clasped his hands around my ankle. I didn't dare to look back. I used the same technique I had used on the were-dragon just a short time before. I lashed out with my other foot, scraping at his hands as hard as I could. I felt the pressure on my ankle lessen and I stabbed downward with my free foot, using the heel of the glass slipper as a weapon. I felt it connect and I raised my foot again, slamming it down as hard as I could. The sharp heel did its job, I felt it sink into flesh and I pulled it back out.

I heard a scream of pain and quickly risked looking down from the high window ledge. I saw the Beast's right hand clutching his left, which was dripping with blood. I looked down to the ground. A finger lay there, all ragged where I had severed it from the hand.

Oopsy—I had done it again.

CHAPTER 56

"Jump, Brina, jump." I recognized Rory's voice and I took a leap of faith into the dark night.

Then, I was falling.

And falling.

And falling. I started to scream. Where were Ruggy and Rory?

"Oh no, we're at the wrong window," I heard Olive shriek. "I can hear her. She's over there!" As I kept falling and screaming, I could hear them arguing and then, when I was about one foot from the ground, they zoomed underneath me and I landed heavily on them.

"Why do people keep landing on me?" I heard Rory's muffled voice asking as I rolled off him.

"Let's get out of here fast," I said as I sat up. "I just accidentally cut one off one of the Beast's fingers ... again."

Ruggy stalled in mid-air. I could feel the eyes of the other two looking for me in the darkness, but decided to gloss over it. I'd worry about it later.

"He's going to be pretty mad," I said casually, "so yeah, we'd better get going. Hey, where are the others?" In answer to my question, Rory told Ruggy to giddy up and we swooped up into the air, leaving our stomachs a long way behind us. Olive gave a little retching noise and held her stomach.

"Are you OK?" I said. She shook her head, then changed her mind and nodded it, deciding to put on a brave face.

"I've just been a bit nauseous since we came back to Dralfynia, but I feel OK really," she said. Ruggy suddenly darted forward in the direction of something that gleamed white ahead of us.

As we drew closer, I could make it out, shining in the moonlight. It was a swan—a huge, beautiful, graceful swan, large enough for Persis, Aidan and Ellie to be squashed onto its back. But that wasn't the strange thing. The really strange thing was that the swan had three necks and three heads. I waved at Aidan to let him know I was all right, but he ignored me.

"Hey," I called out. He stared all around, looking for me. "I'm on Ruggy," I said, then remembered I still had on the glass slippers. I clicked the bows, pulled them off again, and hoped very much that I would never have to wear them again. I waved again as we drew closer and this time he waved back, grinning broadly.

"You have the most exciting adventures," he said. He introduced us to the swan.

"These are the White Widows," he said. "Peggy, LuAnne and Muriel. I thought they were a myth, just a story told to children at bedtime—but here they are, in real life." I wasn't sure I thought this was real life but Aidan was very excited to be meeting his childhood heroines. As he spoke, he kept looking at the magnificent creature and smiling and shaking his head. As we flew on into the ever-darkening night, Aidan told us the White Widows' tale. It was very sad. He explained that they were three beautiful sisters who had married the three handsomest men in the land. But on their wedding day, their new husbands had joined the army, eager to defend their land against another kingdom. After hearing the news of their husbands' deaths in battle, the sisters had wept for three days and three nights, creating a lake of tears. That lake was Lake Pleasant. In its center was the Island of Merthyr and on its banks was Tylwyth Teg.

After they had run out of tears, they had awoken to find they were a single, great swan. The myth was, he said, that if the widows ever sang, it meant war was coming. Their muteness was a symbol of peace.

"That's pretty amazing," I said. "I sure hope they don't sing any time between now and dawn."

"I think we only have about eight hours until dawn tomorrow," said Olive. The beautiful story had taken our minds off what faced us as time ticked by. "That means we don't have long to get the antidote to Witchy Wu's spell and then get to the Island of Merthyr."

"I'm sure that'll be enough time and we'll be fine," I said. I didn't have much conviction in my voice. "Just as long as nothing else goes wrong."

As we flew, I kept close to Rory. He'd always been scared of the dark, ever since he was a little boy. He used to say that witches and monsters came up to his window and looked in and he still slept with a nightlight. Now I wondered if they weren't nightmares at all. Perhaps I should have listened to him.

From time to time we caught sight of the white patches on Clyde, and his gleaming horn, and he galloped below us across the dark land. Rory snuggled into me.

"My fur hurts," he whispered. "I wish I was a boy again."

"It won't be long now," I told him. "We'll be home soon," I promised. "Then Dad can look after you." He nodded his head.

"And Bridget," he said.

"Yes, and Bridget," I agreed. She was pretty good at taking care of us when we fell sick.

"I wonder where we are?" Rory asked. I looked down and sighed.

"I think we're here."

CHAPTER 57

I was right, we had arrived. We had flown to the heart of Scary Forest and now we were circling the clearing where the remains of the gingerbread cottage stood. We had expected to see a ruined pile of crumbs, abandoned to the forest. Instead we saw that Witchy Wu did indeed have bakers in, just as Meera had said, and she was standing right there, making them work through the night.

She was back in her black silk robe and as she strode around her home, I saw that she was still limping from where I had tripped her on the stairs back home. There were several men and women fitting spun-sugar windows and attaching brightly-colored candy buttons and swirl-ing pink and white marshmallows to the walls. Others piped huge swags of white icing, staggering under the weight of the enormous icing bags. They all wore safety helmets made from polished wood.

Ruggy and the White Widows let us down a few yards away in an area where the road through Scary Forest widened slightly and, apart from Persis, we climbed off, stretching our legs and bending our backs to work out some of the stiffness we felt.

We had a fast, whispered conversation. We knew that some of us would have to creep up to find out what was going on before we could start to look for the potion, while some would have to stay behind to take care of the sleeping Persis as well as guarding Ruggy and the White Widows.

I told Rory and Ellie to stay and wait for Clyde. I thought Rory would be happier in the dark if Clyde was with him. I hated to leave him with someone I didn't know but Olive, Aidan and I couldn't wait. It wasn't long until dawn. We began to make our way through the forest. Aidan was really getting into having adventures now and said that he didn't want to be left behind. I guess nothing much very exciting had happened to him until we had arrived and turned the Beast with Nine Fingers into the Beast with Eight—and now Seven—Fingers.

Scary Forest deserved its name, especially in the dead of night. Each step had to be taken carefully so that we wouldn't snap a twig or trip over a branch. We heard leaves rustling as nocturnal animals went about their business. I forced the memory of the bats that had attacked us from my mind. Even our breathing sounded too loud in the darkness.

We came to a stop at the edge of the clearing where the gingerbread cottage stood and hid behind some bushes to watch all the comings and goings. The scene was lit by small fires dotted around. The building site itself was cordoned off by small, bright-orange sherbet cones with licorice ropes strung between them. We read a sign which said that there was danger of falling honeycomb chunks and hard hats had to be worn.

The builders seemed to be exhausted. One fell to his knees as he buckled under the weight of a huge taffy apple. Witchy Wu ordered some of the others to drag him away and dump him in the trees. His voice drifted across to us.

"Please," he begged. "I need the work. My family is starving. The taxes …" his voice trailed to nothing as he was lugged away.

"I don't remember it being so big, do you?" I asked Olive.

"I think she's remodeling," she said. "I like those colored-glass windows she's putting in," she added.

"Mmm. And there's a lot more icing than last time. Looks great. And yummy," I agreed.

"The antidote to the potion?" prodded Aidan. Oh yes, that was what we were there for. Now, I mused, if I were a wicked witch who was remodeling her gingerbread cottage, where would I store all my magic potions while the re-baking work was going on?

There was only one other building nearby. It was a rickety-looking little hut with a single door, one shuttered window and a roof made from planks of wood lain flat.

"All her stuff must be stored in there," I whispered. "That wasn't there before, though."

"I think that it's providing a, um, facility for the builders," Aidan explained. "You know, they are on the building site for a long time and they have to … well, go … if you understand me."

Seriously, why were there so many bathrooms in this particular saga?

"You really think she'd keep her spell stuff in a bathroom?" I asked.

"My mom and dad have a medicine cabinet in their bathroom," pointed out Olive. Aidan stared.

"Your parents have their own bathroom, just for them?" he asked. Olive changed the subject, embarrassed at how much she had compared to the people of Tylwyth Teg.

"I'm certain it's in there," she said confidently. "OK Aidan, you keep a watch and Brina and I will sneak across to get it."

"Why are you coming with me?" I asked.

"Because I'm Goldilocks," she said. "There won't be just one bottle to choose from, will there? There'll be lots. Choosing the one that's just right? That's what I do."

CHAPTER 58

I didn't bother with the glass slippers this time. They hurt too much and if Olive was with me and visible, there didn't seem much point. I had brought them with me in my bag, but I handed the bag to Aidan instead.

"Just in case we get caught," I said casually. "You can take these and Ruggy with you to the Island of Merthyr, so, you know, they'll be safe from the Beast." He took them silently. I hoped that he knew I didn't mean it. I hoped he knew that if Olive and I got caught, he would have to come rescue us and forget all about the stupid slippers.

We waited until Witchy Wu went to the other side of her cottage so she wouldn't see us. There was a huge cauldron over a fire there. It was being used to melt the chocolate used to glue candies onto the roof and walls. The smell was overpoweringly sweet. I had never believed people who tell kids that you can have too much of a good thing but perhaps they had a point after all. This much chocolate was chocolate overload.

Witchy Wu was yelling at the person who was stirring the mixture. "That's too hot, you idiot," she shouted. "Can't you see the cream and the chocolate are separating? Here," she said, snatching the huge wooden spoon, "let me do it."

"Come on, let's go," Olive and I said at the same time. We bent low and scuttled like crabs across the clearing, hoping that the darkness would give us enough cover. I thought that she would follow me, but she obviously thought that I would follow her. We moved along shoulder to shoulder and glared at each other. When we got to the wooden hut, we both tried to go through the door at the same time and got stuck in the doorway. This was becoming a habit for me.

"Let me through," Olive hissed. I stepped back slightly and she fell forward, landing on her hands and knees.

"You told me to let you through," I pointed out as I helped her back up. She dusted off her palms and the skirt of her dress and we looked around us. It was very dark in there.

"Do you think there are rats in here?" I asked as we waited for our eyes to adjust to the gloom.

"Let's just find what we need and get out before rats become a problem," said Olive grumpily. I heard a bang and an "ouch". Then I heard some fumbling and rustling. Was that a rat? Maybe a giant rat? I heard the sound of creaking wood and I froze on the spot. Was someone coming in to the hut?

An orange light filled the hut and I could make out the shape of Olive rubbing her head, standing by a square cut into the wall. On the ground I saw a wooden shutter. She had knocked it off the window as she moved about but at least we could see pretty well by the firelight from outside. She grabbed my arm and pointed through the dim light. Sure enough, fixed to the wall was a large, wooden cupboard. It was shallow and had a pretty double door with wavy edges. Instead of handles, it had small hearts cut out. It seemed too lovely to be a cupboard full of spells in a stinky bathroom, but then this was a witch who lived in a very ornate gingerbread cottage. Olive hooked her fingers into the cut-out hearts and pulled the doors open.

We looked at eight narrow shelves, each one filled with glass bottles of all shapes and sizes and colors. Not one of them was labeled.

I picked up a clear bottle with a cork in it. It was the prettiest shape: slender at the neck and then swooping out to a wide base, and lovely flowers and leaves were etched into the glass. I pulled out the cork and sniffed. Such a beautiful bottle must contain a wonderful cologne.

Bleagh. It smelled like a laundry basket. I went to sniff again just to make sure, but Olive smacked my hand.

"What are you doing?" she said. "This stuff is dangerous." Then she gasped and cried out, "Brina! Your head's shrunk."

CHAPTER 59

I patted myself up and down to see what she meant. To my dismay, my head was very tiny but my body around my hips had swelled right out. I was exactly the same shape as the bottle I had sniffed.

No! This could not be happening to me! I was horrified and mad at myself for doing such a dumb thing just as the end to this whole saga was in sight.

"What shall I do?" my very tiny head squeaked to Olive. She was standing there, shaking her head in disbelief.

"Why did you sniff that stuff?" she asked. I tried to shrug, but my shoulders were so narrow that I just rocked from side to side. I tried to take a step. Because my body was so wide, I couldn't see my feet anymore, but I could still feel them. Unfortunately, my legs and feet had shrunk so much that I could only manage a very little step. I reached out to the cupboard. There must be an antidote. My arms were too short to reach the cupboard and they flapped around pointlessly in mid-air. I couldn't stay like this! What if dawn came and I got sent back to Melas shaped like a bottle? I couldn't ever cycle to school again; my legs weren't long enough to reach the pedals. My earbuds would never fit into ears as tiny as mine, so no music. And my fingers were now so stubby I couldn't even manage a remote control so no TV either.

"Do something," I told Olive, panic in my voice.

"Like … ?" she asked.

"I don't know. Find me an antidote," I said, then added 'please,' so she knew I was serious.

"Hm, I'm not sure," she said. "I might need Aidan to help me. Shall I go get him?" She was enjoying herself.

"No!" I almost yelled in alarm. "Just practice your Goldilocks thing and chose the one that's just right, OK?" I would have tried for a pitiful, puppy-eyed, begging look but my eyes were now the size of dots. Chuckling, she turned back to the cupboard and stood in front of the dozens of bottles, pinching her lower lip while she thought. She lifted her hand and let it trail along the bottles, talking to herself as she went.

"This one feels too big; this one feels too small; too salty, yuk; too bland; too hard; too soft—no, wait. This one feels just right." She took a bottle that was dark green glass, weighed it in her hand for a moment then gave a sharp nod.

"Yes this one; this is definitely the antidote." Oh thank goodness. I took a very small step toward her so she could hand me the bottle, but she snatched it away.

"This isn't for you," she said. "This is Persis' antidote."

"What about me?" I moaned. She shrugged. Shrugging was just a memory for me now and I was envious of her shoulders.

"I don't think I can help with that," she admitted. "I can help you choose a chair or a bed that's just right if you like?"

"What? No, I don't want a bed or a chair, and don't even think about offering me any type of breakfast cereal. Just help me get back to normal," I said.

"You mean 'normal'," she giggled, hooking the first two fingers of each hand to show speech marks. I glared at her.

"Just. Do. Something," I begged. She shrugged again. Now she was just showing off her shrugging skills.

"I'm just kidding you," she told me. "You turned back to normal a minute ago. I looked down. I was never so happy to see my feet again—yay! I tried a shrug. Both my shoulders went up and down. Yes! I was the same shape that I always was.

"OK, let's get out of here," I said. Then a thought occurred to me. These bottles all contained spells or potions. Even if we didn't know what they did, they might be useful on our way to the Island of Merthyr. I grabbed a couple, stuffed them into my pockets and then we creaked open the door a tiny fraction of an inch at a time until it was wide enough to look through.

A semicircle of wolves sat outside the hut, watching and waiting. They had polished-wood helmets on their heads. One of them licked its lips with a long, pink, drippy tongue. In the center of them stood Witchy Wu.

CHAPTER 60

I shut the door again.

"Maybe they didn't notice us," I said.

"I think you shut the door pretty fast," agreed Olive. "And perhaps there's a way out at the back." But there wasn't. This was the Dralfynian version of a porta-potty. Yes it was bigger, yes it was wooden and not plastic, and yes it had a medicine cupboard full of spells and potions, but there was still no back door.

"Maybe they've gotten fed up of waiting and gone away," I said. "Shall I look again?"

"Aarrrooooooooo."

"I think they're still out there."

"Do you think she just wants to capture us? We're pretty good at being captured and then escaping," I said hopefully.

"Aarrrooooooooo."

"No. I think she wants the wolves to eat us."

Eaten by wolves? I wasn't even a teenager yet—I was too young to be eaten by wolves. And it seemed like it would be painful.

"I don't like the sound of that," I said nervously.

"Me neither," said Olive.

"What shall we do?" But before she could answer, help arrived in the shape of an adorable ginger bear cub, an enormous unicorn and an inn-keeper's son. We heard a great disturbance coming from outside.

"Woohoo," I heard Aidan yelling. Clyde had obviously caught up with the rest of them and when Aidan saw we were trapped, he had gone for help.

The three of them shouted, neighed and roared and we heard the wolves howling in reply. Olive yanked at my arm.

"Come on," she said. "Just run. Don't look around to see what's happening. Just run. Head for the White Widows: if we get separated, we'll meet there."

I kicked open the door, ignored her advice not to look around and saw that the wolves were loping across the clearing to the edge of the woods. I caught sight of trampled bushes where the others had crashed through as they ran away. Witchy Wu was limping along following the pack. The building site was almost deserted and I realized that she had cast a spell that changed her bakers into a wolf pack, hard hats and all. I twisted my body and headed away from them. I hoped I could circle back around and find the White Widows and Ruggy after I had escaped. I picked up speed and ignored my sore feet and ankle— I just felt thankful that my legs were the normal length again.

In seconds I was across the clearing, hurdling over the rope of licorice and burst through the trees. I was so afraid of the wolves that I didn't have enough fear left to be scared of tripping, of making a noise or of the snuffling animals that were hiding between the trees. I charged through the woods and any of the creatures I had been so afraid of before now scattered to avoid me treading on them. My lungs were bursting and I thought I had probably come far enough to be fairly safe.

I slowed down and turned to tell Olive we should veer around to where the meeting point was. The forest was silent and dark. She wasn't there. Either she hadn't followed me, or she hadn't been able to keep up.

"Olive?" I called out softly. "Olive are you there?"

"Who?" said a voice above my head. I looked up, startled, but it was just an owl. "Hoo," it repeated.

I just had to hope that she would do the same as I planned to do: head to where the White Widows were waiting. I leaned against the tree to catch my breath before I started off.

"Yew again," said the tree. I jumped two feet from the ground. Despite being a tree, Russell somehow managed to appear at the times when we needed him most. "I thought you might need some help, but I was stumped about what to do, so I came over to see what was happening."

I told him that, although we were at last on our way to the Island of Merthyr, Witchy Wu and her pack of wolves were chasing Rory, Aidan and Clyde.

"Climb up, my little seedling," said Russell. "Let's make sure you all leaf Scary Forest in one piece."

I clambered up a few branches until I was high above the ground and waited for Russell to move. I had forgotten how slowly trees move. I heard the sound of the ground ripping and smelled fresh earth as we lurched forward at an unhurried pace. It was a bouncy ride and I had to wrap my arms around his trunk to keep from falling. Although it took a long time to get there, we didn't have to go far to find the others—we just followed the horrible sounds of howling and yelping and screaming.

Olive and Aidan had their backs to a tree, just an ordinary, unmagical tree. Rory and Clyde were in front of them, protecting them. Rory was bleeding from a wound on his shoulder. Whenever a wolf from the pack charged at them, Clyde reared up then brought his great hooves down, usually missing the wolf by only a whisker. Rory was lashing out with his claws, snarling and showing his sharp teeth but they were badly outnumbered and it was just a matter of time before the wolves overran them.

I think the sight of his friends being attacked and hurt enraged Russell. He let out a great roar, and flung his branches up high, accidentally flinging me to the ground. I staggered to my feet and stood on trembling legs. The pack of wolves turned at the sound and spotted me. I was alone and unprotected.

The biggest wolf of all (of course!) began a low growl that made my skin shiver. He dropped low and began to crawl toward me. Saliva dripped from his mouth and his red-rimmed eyes were fixed on me. He was so close, I could feel his hot breath on my skin. My mouth was dry. I couldn't drag my gaze away from him to look for a weapon in case he lunged at me. My legs felt so weak that I could hardly move. I managed a step back to be closer to Russell, hoping I would find the strength to climb back up. Surely he would help me? I couldn't believe that Russell would just dump me in the middle of a pack of wolves without any help.

He hadn't.

CHAPTER 61

His terrific roar had resonated throughout the forest, sending a message that rebounded off the trees. It had been heard by a pair of creatures who were already out and searching nearby. Two enormous bears burst through the undergrowth, batting aside thorny thickets of brambles and small trees as if they were nothing more than paper. They took one look at a bear cub being attacked by a pack of wolves, stood on their hind legs and bellowed as loud as thunder. They stood as tall as a truck and their teeth were long and cruelly sharp. Then they charged, sweeping the wolves aside with their huge paws as if they were leaves, sending them flying through the air and crashing into the bushes nearby. Their hard hats did nothing to protect them.

The wolves knew when they were beaten; they snapped and snarled, but in the end, they slunk away, still growling and looking back at us with malice in their faces.

The pack did not disappear completely. They stopped nearby and regrouped, licking their wounds and staring at us. I could see half a dozen pairs of scarlet eyes, and then I noticed one pair that was green and black. Witchy Wu had caught up with her pack of wolves. I moved over to stand with the others. We waited silently. Something was coming. Were they going to attack again?

Witchy Wu gave a slight smile which turned my tummy to water. She raised her arms in the air. In one hand she held her stick. Now it fizzed at the tip like a sparkler.

"On this night of a full moon," she chanted. We exchanged uneasy glances. That sounded like the start of a spell.

"Summon a dragon and bring her soon," she continued. It sounded like she was telling Latrina Earwax where we were. We had escaped her once, but I didn't think our luck would hold for a second time. I did the only thing I could think of. I took one of the bottles of spells from my pocket and I threw it right at her.

It landed at her feet, shattered into a hundred pieces and released a cloud of purple smoke. Witchy Wu screamed and ran backward. As she did, her head, legs and arms started to shrink and her hips ballooned out. It was the same bottle that I had sniffed before. Although her arms were very short, her magic wand was still as long. She waved it around and a spark flashed from it, chasing away the purple smoke. She waved it again and she returned to normal. Then she stopped being normal and started to grow. In two seconds, she was as tall as the bears; in three she was as tall as Russell. Her fingernails stretched and sharpened until she had talons as sharp as the were-dragon's.

She had moved further away to be out of throwing distance. Wishing I had Persis with her strength and accuracy to hand over to, I did the next best thing and passed the second bottle to Aidan. I figured that he might have the strength to throw it a greater distance than I could manage—he had dealt with the pails full of milk much easier than I had (I didn't bother with Olive; I had seen her play sports at school). He took it from me, got Witchy Wu squarely in his sights and hurled the bottle. It landed smack on the witch's head where it broke, releasing a billow of red smoke.

The wolf pack scattered. Whatever was in the two bottles was too much for them. As the smoke cleared, we saw Witchy Wu starting to shrink. She dropped her wand to rub her eyes which were red and sore where the smoke had irritated them. I couldn't understand why she was making such a big fuss. It was as if she was scared to close them and let tears rinse away the smoke. Her skin turned red and shiny with the effort of not crying and then she gave a sob. One single, sad tear slid down her cheek and dropped to the ground, sizzling as it hit the cold earth. She bent and picked up her wand, her whole body shaking with fury and hatred. She glared at me with complete loathing, then turned her back on us and started hobbling after the wolves.

"She'll be back," said Aidan. "We only have a few minutes to get out of here before she recovers and comes after us." I nodded and turned to tell the others.

I saw that the two bears had dropped to all fours and ambled over to Rory. They had begun to nuzzle and lick him.

"Hey, quit it," he said, which I thought it was a bit ungrateful considering they had just saved his life. Then the smaller of the two bears picked Rory up by the scruff of his neck so that he swung there like a kitten being carried by a momma cat.

They turned and started to leave, taking Rory with them.

I ran after them.

"That's my brother," I called out. "He's not really Baby Bear." They turned around to look at me, making poor Rory rock backward and forward.

"You're barking up the wrong tree with that cub, my friends," agreed Russell. The two bears looked at each other and the one holding Rory opened her mouth, sending Rory plummeting down to the ground. He landed with a thud and groaned. The mother bear spat some of his fur from her mouth.

"But thanks anyway," I told their backs as they went on their way. It felt like an anti-climax after the sheer terror of the wolf attack.

Olive came up to me.

"We need to go," she said. She pointed upwards. The moon had already traveled a long way across the sky. It was well past midnight and dawn was only few hours away.

We all gave Russell a hasty farewell hug, although Rory paused long enough to say, "I hope you don't get in trouble for helping us; I'd hate for you to be accused of treeson." Then we ran to where the White Widows, Ellie and Persis were still waiting.

"What was all that noise?" asked Ellie. "It was really scary here." I left Aidan to fill her in, while Olive and I went to the White Widows. One of them bent her neck back to watch us, then she rubbed her head on Persis. They were worried about her. Olive passed me the dark green bottle and I took out the cork. Immediately, tendrils of a very familiar green smoke poured out, twining around the bottle and my hand.

"I think you picked the bottle that contains the poisoned spell, not the antidote," I said. "This is the same stuff that was in Rory's bedroom when Witchy Wu sent you and Persis to sleep." Olive shook her head stubbornly.

"No," she said. "I know that it's that bottle. Give it time." As we watched, the wisps of smoke drifted across the back of the White Widows to Persis. They began to coil around her, slowly at first then faster and faster. They wrapped her from head to toe in a soft mist so that we couldn't even see her. For what felt like ages nothing happened. Then, the mist started to evaporate, disappearing into the night. Persis stretched. She yawned. She sat up.

"Why are you guys all looking at me?" she said. Then she looked down. "Am I lying on a feather bed?" she asked. One of the White Widows turned back and crossly snapped her beak at Persis.

"Ah, no. You're on a giant swan with three heads in the middle of Scary Forest and we really have to go," I said rapidly. Olive and I climbed onto the back of the White Widows and I saw that Aidan, Rory and Ellie were already seated on Ruggy. Clyde pawed at the ground and gave a whinny. He wanted to be on his way. He kept looking at the direction the wolves had run.

"Up, up and away, I guess," I said. The White Widows rose to their webbed feet and flapped their vast wings a couple of times—the draft made Clyde stagger—and then we were all on our way. This was the last leg of our journey. Soon we would be on the Island of Merthyr. Everyone would be safe, including the magic objects. Then the rest of us could go home.

CHAPTER
62

King Michael and Queen Hazel lived in a big, messy log cabin with a lot of cats. There were other buildings where their servants and the islanders lived, but the overall impression was of cats.

A lot of cats.

There were skinny Siamese and fluffy Persians; there were cats that were black, white, gray, ginger, tabby and some were strange combinations of them all. Some of the cats were very old, others had been injured and lost a limb or an eye or their tail. All were well-fed, loved and happy.

The king and queen insisted we call them Michael and Hazel instead of Your Majesty. They listened to our tales and reluctantly took Ruggy and the glass slippers when I forced them into their hands.

"We hoped we had left that world behind when we came here," sighed Michael. He put his hand on his wife's knee. They looked troubled.

"It's not possible to escape the evil that people do," she said.

Yeah, especially when it's your own son who's responsible, I thought.

"We have to do the right thing, my dear," said Hazel. "We will offer sanctuary to the girl Ellie, and our protection to the rug and the slippers."

"Is that all?" I asked. The rude words slipped out before I could stop them. They stared at me.

"What else can we do?"

"I don't know; help your people somehow, maybe?" I said.

"Child, our hearts were broken when we lost our daughter," Michael told me.

"I know that it's hard to lose someone; I lost my mom," I answered. "But you still have to go on. There's still stuff you have to do. If Princess Heidi was anything like my mom, I know she'd want you to stop her brother taking over Dralfynia."

I stood there, staring at them, looking a lot braver than I felt. But I had come through a lot and I couldn't stand to think it might be wasted. The people loved their king and queen. I hoped my words would make them love their people.

Later on, we sat in a big room filled with cozy chairs and a roaring fire. Persis, Aidan and I had eaten bread and cheese; Rory had eaten honey and Olive had finally had her porridge. We were waiting now: waiting for dawn, waiting to go back home. Persis was still complaining about being exhausted. Rory's fur still hurt and Olive still felt sick all the time. Something about this saga had made them all ill and I wondered what it was. Aidan came to join us.

"I have to go back," he said. "There's a lot to do. Clyde is on the shore, waiting for me. I'll row across."

"What's going to happen now?" I asked. He shook his head.

"I don't know," he said. "Maybe nothing. Maybe Princess Heidi will come forward, or her heirs if she has any, and we will be safe." His words had no hope in them. I suddenly gave him a hug. At least this time, I could say goodbye and thank him.

He hugged me back.

"You saved Ellie," he said. "And with two of the magic objects here, it stops the Beast taking power for now. Thank you." As I watched him go,

I didn't feel as though I had done any good at all. I felt as though I was causing more trouble, and then turning my back on my responsibilities and leaving a mess for someone else to clean up. Just like last time.

I watched Aidan climb into a little row boat and start his journey. As I did, the sky became lighter and streaks of orange began to appear on the low horizon.

I went back to Rory and the others and said, "It's time." They stood up and we found Hazel waiting behind us.

"I'll show you where," she told us. We walked quickly from the house and across a lawn covered in yellow patches of dead grass—a consequence of all those cats. We passed through a gate and along a winding, sandy path. Hazel sped up as the morning grew lighter and lighter.

Then she stopped. Ahead of her was an expanse of gray mud. It bubbled and popped. It looked like a living thing. I sniffed. It smelled like rotten eggs and I wrinkled my nose.

"Be careful," she warned us. "It's boiling hot. If anything falls into the mud, it has no chance of surviving. It's one of the reasons we chose this island to retire to; it makes it difficult to attack."

Hazel laid her hand on my arm and looked at me.

"Your words touched us, my dear," she said. "If your mother was anything like our daughter, she would want you to do the right thing, always. And you have."

Then she pointed beyond the hot mud to a pool that was surrounded by rushes and filled with clear, fresh water. It steamed gently and the rising sun colored it orange and red.

"The hot spring will be the best place for you to return to your land," she said. "It reaches deep into the earth and is the purest water on Merthyr."

As we walked across to it, I groped with my fingers into my pocket. After all this time and all we had been through, the bottle that Bridget had given to Olive was still there, although we wouldn't need it.

Then a sound filled the air and our ears and our brains. It was pure and beautiful, a single note that went on and on.

It was the most frightening sound I had ever heard.

Hazel grasped my hand, her fingers closing on mine.

"Oh my dear child," she said. "It's the White Widows. They are singing."

CHAPTER 63

O ur journey back was sudden. One minute we were standing next to the hot spring listening to the haunting song of the White Widows, the next we were being pulled into the vortex that would take us back to Melas. It was different this time. I found myself flat on my back, spinning like a top while the hot steam swirled around me. It smelled foul and I began to sweat from the heat. And then, as we had every time, we landed with a thud, gasping and shaking. We were back in our cubicle in the girls' bathroom at school.

We hoped.

It was so dark that we couldn't see anything. We all stretched out our hands at the same time and straight away bumped into each other.

"That's my nose," complained Persis.

"Sorry, I thought it was the latch on the door," I apologized. "Everyone else stand still; I'll go switch on the lights." I found my way carefully to the light switch after bumping into the sinks and the trash can on the way. I clicked the switch and the room was flooded with a brilliant, cold light. We all blinked and covered our eyes until we adjusted.

It was completely silent.

"I think this place is totally empty," said Rory. "I wonder what time it is?"

"I wonder what day it is," added Olive. "I hope we're not in trouble."

Of course we were in trouble. When we ran to the school's front door, hoping to sneak out and get home without being seen, our movement set off the alarms. The doors were locked and all we could do was stand and watch helplessly as Principal McPhail and a police officer came to let us out.

It was the early hours of the day after our detention. Our story was that we had run away from Ms. Wu because we were afraid of her, found Rory waiting for us, and had hidden from her. We said we had fallen asleep while we were waiting for it to be safe to leave. When Principal McPhail tried to contact Witchy Wu to ask what had happened and why she hadn't reported the disappearance of her entire detention class, he couldn't reach her. In the end, after a totally unnecessary amount of fuss, the grown-ups had to believe us.

It was almost daybreak by the time I helped Bridget put Rory to bed. When she saw the marks where the wolves had attacked him and the wounds on my ankle, she had made a brown ointment that smelled gross but we did feel better afterwards.

Rory was asleep in seconds. We stood and watched him. He had been a cute bear cub, and he was a cute kid—when he was asleep. I turned to go to my own room, but Bridget laid a hand on my arm to stop me.

"Sabrina," she said. "When you have slept there are things we need to talk about. Things that it is time for you to know," she said to me. I nodded.

"I think I already know," I said briefly.

I was exhausted. I went to bed and dreamed of giant bears wearing crowns and dancing. Then the image changed to hordes of blue-skinned goblins swarming over a map of Dralfynia and Twinkle was a drawing in the map, hissing and fighting them. Then it shifted again and I saw a dragon fighting a swan with three necks while, on the ground below, I sat reading a book and pretending I couldn't hear the pain-filled cries of the swan. When I woke up, I felt more tired than when I had gone to bed. I dragged myself up, dressed and grabbed a banana for myself and an apple for Clyde. It was early in the afternoon and the rest of the kids in Melas were at school. I left the house, blinking in the bright daylight. I crossed the road and climbed the fence to Clyde's field.

He wasn't there. Somehow, I wasn't surprised. I had hoped to see him, but in truth I didn't know if he would ever come back. Dralfynia was on the brink of war. He would be needed there, not watching over Rory and me. My bottom lip trembled. I didn't want Clyde to be gone. I missed him. I even missed his farts. He had been my friend since we moved to our house. Since my mom had left us and then died.

Or since whatever had really happened to her. I had been lied to a lot. I had trusted the wrong person. After my two adventures I had begun to understand a few things, like why only Rory and I could see Twinkle and drive Ruggy, and why only I could wear the magic slippers. I began to understand the unspoken words that had hung between Hazel and me.

There was a footstep behind me.

"Hello, Sabrina."

I recognized the voice. It was the Beast. He was in Melas. He had followed us from Dralfynia.

"Hello," I replied.

EPILOGUE

Duchess Yvonne stood in front of Meera. She combed out her long gray hair and for the time being, Meera was silent. Through a crack in the wall, a mouse in a purple velvet jacket crept into the duchess' chamber. The mouse watched the duchess silently then tilted its head, smiling as it heard a noise from the corridor beyond. The mouse knew what was coming.

The door to the room was flung violently open.

"Nephew," said the duchess. "How dare you force your way into my room. It's very rude, you know. Mind you, I always said your mother didn't discipline you enough. And what are the palace guards doing here?"

"Aunty Yvonne," said Prince Donaldo. "I'm afraid you're under arrest for helping the known traitor Cinderella escape. I'll be taking full control of the kingdom immediately." He tried to click his fingers—but, as he was missing three on one hand, he made only a soft shushing sound. The guards knew what he meant anyway. They entered the room and gripped the duchess by her arms.

"Take her to the dungeon," said the Beast. "Since your friends caused my tower to be destroyed, you will have to take your chances with the other prisoners. Oh, and Aunty?" he called, as the guards dragged her away. "I'll be popping over to see dear old Mother and Father soon. Once I collect the Royal Magic Objects from them, there will be nothing to stop me becoming king."

Deep in Scary Forest, a mommy bear and a daddy bear found their own lost bear cub, sleeping under a pile of fall leaves. From her hiding place, a homeless girl with loop-de-loop braids watched and waited. She knew that if she followed them, they would lead her to their house and offer her food and a warm place to sleep.

Inside a tower in a nearby kingdom, a princess slept soundly. She was having the strangest dreams—but it would still be many years before she would awaken.

And a prince, who was very charming, woke with a start on his throne. He was bored with a life of going to balls and dances and tea parties. Suddenly he craved adventure and drama. Suddenly he wanted to make a difference.

In a shop in Timaru, a puppet-maker was at work. His window was full of beautifully carved walking sticks and amazing puppets hanging from their strings. He was working on a short piece of wood, sanding it and shaping it carefully. He held it to the light and admired it. It was perfect copy of a human finger. He passed it to his client.

"I think this will match the others well, Your Highness," he said.

"Thank you, Bill," the Beast replied. He fitted the wooden finger to his hand and wriggled it. Whenever he traveled between lands, he wore his wooden fingers. Along with his mustache, they were an important part of his disguise.

ABOUT THE AUTHOR

Michele Clark McConnochie has worked in education as a teacher and manager for over 20 years. These days, she is also a freelance writer and creative writing teacher who lives in Christchurch, New Zealand with her husband Brent, her step-daughter Steph, and their two very spoilt rescue cats, Twinkle and Cleo. She supports Wolverhampton Wanderers Football Club and likes Dr. Who, Snoopy, chocolate and reading. Her favorite book when she was young was 'Little Women.'

Did you know that there are lots of types of entertainment that are cruel to animals, just like the goblins were to Rory? If you are looking for something fun to do, there are heaps of great ideas that aren't cruel.

Did you know that animal rescue centers around the world have heaps of animals who desperately need a place to live? If you are looking for a pet and can provide a kind, loving home, why not check out your nearest animal shelter, just like Queen Hazel and King Michael do?

And if you would like to contact Michele, she would be thrilled to hear from you.

Visit   www.MCMauthor.com,   follow   her   on   Facebook   at facebook.com/micheleclarkmcconnochie, or follow her on Twitter @ MicheleClarkMcC.

If you want to read more about the people of Dralfynia, you can sign up to Michele's newsletter and you will get receive a free e-book, Tales from Dralfynia! Go to www.MCMauthor.com to find out more.

CPSIA information can be obtained
at www.ICGtesting.com
Printed in the USA
LVHW032041110320
649750LV00001B/7